The Suns of Independence

The Suns of Independence

AHMADOU KOUROUMA

Translated from the French by
Adrian Adams

AFRICANA PUBLISHING COMPANY

NEW YORK

First published in the United States of America 1981 by
Africana Publishing Company,
an imprint of Holmes & Meier Publishers, Inc.
160 Broadway, New York, NY 10038

© Les Presses de l'Université de Montréal 1968

Translation copyright © 1981 by Adrian Adams
First published by Les Presses de l'Université de Montréal, 1968

Library of Congress Cataloging in Publication Data

Kourouma, Ahmadou.
    The suns of independence.

    Translation of Les soleils des indépendances.
    I. Title.
PQ3989.2.K58S613   1981   843   80-8891

ISBN 0-8419-0747-1

Printed in the United States of America

Contents

The Suns of Independence

PART ONE

1 *The mastiff and his shameless way of sitting*

One week had passed since Ibrahima Kone, of the Malinke race, had met his end in the capital city, or to put it in Malinke: he'd been defeated by a mere cold ...

As with every Malinke, once life had fled his remains, his shade rose, spat, dressed and set out on the long journey to its distant native land, there to impart the sad news. On lonely paths far out in the bush, two Malinke pedlars met the shade and recognised it. It was walking fast and did not greet them. They knew straight away what had happened:

'Ibrahima has finished,' they said to themselves.

In its native village, the shade rearranged its belongings, putting them in order. From behind the hut you could hear the deceased's tin trunk banging shut, his calabashes rattling about; even his sheep and goats were restless, and uttered strange cries. Everyone knew what had happened.

'Ibrahima Kone has finished,' they said, 'his shade has come.'

The shade then returned to the city, where lay its remains, to attend the funeral: a round trip of a thousand miles, in the time it takes to wink an eye!

You seem sceptical. Well, I swear it's true, and what is more, I swear that if the deceased had been of blacksmith caste, and if we weren't living in the era of Independence (the suns of Independence, the Malinke say), no one would have dared bury him far away in foreign soil. An elder of the caste would have travelled down from home with a little cane. Once he had tapped the corpse with that cane, the shade would have re-entered the body, and the dead man would have risen. The dead man would have been handed the cane, and he would have followed the elder; they would have walked together day and night. But mind! without the dead

3

man's coming to life! Life is in God's power alone! Without eating,
drinking, speaking or even sleeping the dead man would have
walked until they reached the village, where the elder would have
taken back the cane and tapped him with it again. The shade would
then once more have left the corpse; whereupon the various exceed-
ingly complicated funeral rites for a Malinke of blacksmith caste
would have been performed in his native village.

It is therefore possible, indeed certain, that the shade walked
to its native village, then returned just as quickly to the capital
city in order to conduct the burial; a sorcerer who attended the
funeral saw it sitting on the coffin, looking melancholy. Day after
day followed the burial, until the seventh day came and the
seventh-day funeral rites were performed in the presence of the
shade; then weeks passed until the fortieth day came, and the
fortieth-day funeral rites took place before the seated shade, that
remained invisible to ordinary Malinke. Then the shade took its
leave forever, and walked back to the Malinke homeland, there
to bring joy to a mother through reincarnation as a Malinke
infant.

Because the shade was present, watching, counting, giving
thanks, the burial was piously performed, and the funeral rites
observed with prodigality. Friends, relatives, even mere passers-by
deposited gifts and sacrifices which were then divided up and
shared out among those present and the great Malinke families of
the capital city.

Since every funeral ceremony pays, one can readily understand
why Malinke praise-singers and elderly Malinke, those whose trad-
ing activities were ruined by Independence (and God alone knows
how many old traders ruined by Independence there are in the capital city!) all 'work' the burials and funeral rites. Real professionals!
Morning, noon and night they keep on the move from one neighbourhood to another, in order to attend all the ceremonies. The
Malinke most unkindly refer to them as 'the vultures' or 'that pack
of hyenas'.

Fama Dumbuya! A true Dumbuya, of Dumbuya father and
Dumbuya mother, the last legitimate descendant of the Dumbuya
princes of Horodugu, whose totem was the panther – Fama was
a 'vulture'. A Dumbuya prince! A panther totem in a hyena pack.
Ah! the suns of Independence!

Fama was going to be late for the seventh-day funeral rites of
Ibrahima Kone. Faster and faster he walked, as if seized with diar-

rhoea. He was still at the far end of the bridge linking the white men's town with the African quarter, and it was time for second prayer; the ceremony had begun.

Fama grumbled: 'Hell and damnation! *Nyamokode!*'

Everything conspired to exasperate him. The sun! the sun! the cursed sun of Independence filled half the sky, scorching the universe so as to justify the unhealthy late-afternoon storms. And the people in the street! the bastards lounging about in the middle of the pavement as if it were their old man's backyard. You had to shove, threaten and curse your way past. All this in the midst of an ear-splitting din: horns hooting, motors racing, tyres flapping, passers-by and drivers shouting. Beyond the left-hand railing of the bridge, the lagoon glittered with the blinding flash of many mirrors, shattering and coalescing as far as the distant bank, the ash-grey horizon set with small islands and fringed with forest. The bridge was crowded with many-coloured cars, coming and going; beyond the right-hand railing was the lagoon, still glittering in places, but elsewhere choked with laterite soil; the harbour with its ships and warehouses, the edge of the forest and at last a bit of blue: the sea, soon lost in the blue of the horizon. God be praised! Luckily Fama hadn't much further to walk now; he could see the end of the harbour, over there where the road disappeared in a hollow, where other warehouses, their tin roofs gleaming or dull grey, clustered about palm-trees and clumps of foliage from which emerged a few two-storey houses with shuttered windows. It was an immense disgrace and shame, as great as that of the old panther caught fighting with hyenas over carrion, for Fama to be chasing after funerals in this way.

He, Fama, born to gold, food in plenty, honour and women! Bred to prefer one gold to another, to choose between many dishes, to bed his favourite of a hundred wives! What was he now? A scavenger ... A hyena in a hurry.

The sky remained lofty and clear, except on the seaward side where a few little scattered clouds had begun seeking each other out to make a storm. What a miserable misbegotten time of year it was here, between seasons, mingling sunshine and rain.

After crossing a square, he turned up the central avenue of the government employees' quarter. Praise be to God! It was here all right. But Fama was late, all the same. That was unfortunate; it meant he was going to have flung in his face, and in public, the kind of insulting reproof that's like having a snake in the folds of your trousers: unbearable whether you're standing, sitting, walking or lying down.

In any case, he had arrived. The Julas, the Malinke traders, in their white, blue, green, yellow, let us say many-coloured robes, filled part of the space between the building's pillars; they were all crowded together, arms waving, the palaver in full flow. Ibrahima, dead and buried, had drawn a good crowd for his seventh day! At a glance he could recognise and count ears and noses from all the neighbourhoods and all the professions. Fama greeted the assembly, and with what broad smiles! found a place among the pillars, gathered up the folds of his robe and lowered his tall frame on to the corner of a mat. The wizened old praise-singer who was calling out announcements and comments, replied:

'The prince of Horodugu, the last legitimate Dumbuya, has condescended to join us ... a bit late.'

People looked up with sarcastic smiles. Let's face it: a prince who's practically a beggar is a grotesque figure under any sun. Fama didn't waste his anger insulting those sneering bastards, those sons of dogs. But there was worse to come. The praise-singer continued:

'That he is late, does not matter: the customary rights of noble families have been respected; the Dumbuya have not been forgotten. The princes of Horodugu have been put with the Keita.'

Fama asked the praise-singer to repeat what he had just said. The man hesitated. Those who are not Malinke may not know it: in the circumstances this was a deliberate insult, enough to make your eyeballs explode with rage. Who had lumped Dumbuya and Keita together? The latter are kings of Wasulu, and their totem is the hippopotamus, not the panther.

Once more, his voice firm and resonant with anger, Fama asked the praise-singer to repeat himself. The man launched into a flood of self-justification: symbolic, everything was symbolic in these ceremonies, and people should be content with that; it was a shame, a great shame for custom and religion that some old men in this city had to live off what was handed out at funeral rites ... In other words, a lot of damned nonsense, quite uncalled-for. Bastard of a praise-singer! There were no real praise-singers left; the real ones died with the great masters of war, before the European conquest. Fama was going to have to prove there and then that there were still men alive who wouldn't put up with such bastards. If you pretend, out of discretion, not to notice a shameless man's fart, he'll just assume that you've no sense of smell.

Fama rose, and thundered so the building shook. The praise-singer, disconcerted, no longer knew with what wind to sway. He asked the seated throng to listen and open their ears to the offended, the outraged son of the Dumbuya whose totem is the panther, himself a panther and unable to conceal fury and rage. Then he called out to Fama:

'True descendant of the masters of war! speak out, speak truly! say what ails you! explain the offence! spit out your grievances for all to hear!'

Emboldened by the praise-singer's uneasiness, Fama prepared to launch on a flood of speech: he had the floor, an audience and a just cause. Tell me, what more could a proper Malinke desire? He cleared his throat with a panther's roar, straightened his cap, unfurled the sleeves of his robe, strutted a few paces forward so that everyone might see him, and began his palaver. The praise-singer repeated Fama's words. Fama was shouting, and was about to roar still louder, when ... Damned praise-singer! Damned cough! Seized with an ill-timed violent fit of coughing, the praise-singer was suddenly bent double, hawking his lungs out, and Fama's speech was interrupted. The last of the Dumbuya, who felt not the least sympathy for the praise-singer, was not discouraged; on the contrary, he lowered his gaze to collect his thoughts and remember a few suitable proverbs, and did not look about him. But how could he not feel it? People were tired, they were fed up with Fama's attention-seeking at every gathering, his palavers without head or tail. There was a rustling of robes and mats in the throng, people began to frown and to talk among themselves with emphatic gestures. Always that Fama, always shares that were too small, always something. They had had enough. Make him sit down!

The praise-singer had finally got rid of his cough, but it was too late. The atmosphere was seething with irritation. Fama saw nothing, heard nothing; he talked and talked, long and forcefully, waving his arms like the branches of the silk-cotton tree, plucking proverbs out of thin air, his mouth wry with excitement. Intoxicated, carried away, he could not see that the audience was in a frenzy of restlessness, as if they were being bitten by an army of ants; legs folding and unfolding, hands moving from pocket to chin and chin to pocket; he could not see their faces twisted with anger, nor hear remarks like 'Ah! it's getting late, to hell with it!' bursting forth. The palaver was his.

Suddenly someone shouted from the throng:

'Sit your arse down and shut your mouth! Our ears are tired of hearing you!'

The man who had spoken was short and squat as the stump of a tree, with a stony face and the neck, arms, fists and shoulders of a wrestler; he was trembling with excitement like a cornered cricket, and stood on tiptoe to try and match Fama's height.

'You know no shame, and shame is what counts above all,' he added with a snort.

There was a general uproar, like a herd of buffalo pounding through the forest. The scrawny praise-singer struggled in vain to lay the storm Fama had raised.

'Bamba! (that was the assailant's name) Bamba!' he shouted hoarsely. 'Cool your heart!'

Holding his ground, grinding his jaws like a wild beast, making threatening moves with his elbows, shoulders and head, how could Bamba heed the praise-singer's feeble cries? And how could Fama? Worked up to a quivering rage, he was mouthing curses: that son of a dog Bamba thought he could play the man, did he! He, Fama, would strike him down, throttle him, disgrace him. He strode towards the offender. Only two steps! Fama had scarcely taken two steps when that stocky little Bamba leapt like a dancer, landing right in front of him. Each clutched a fold of the other's robe. The praise-singer vanished, and the uproar grew louder; on all sides people rose to pull them apart; there was a sound of ripped cloth, and they were separated. Fama gathered up his robe and sat down, a bit too quickly. But two strong men were needed to tear Bamba away and drag him back to his place. When the two antagonists had been seated, everyone else sat down.

Fama made his apologies. The oldest man present asked forgiveness for all Muslims on Fama's behalf. Fama was in the right, he declared. The truth must be told, however harsh it may be; it may redden your eyes, but it won't blind you. Consequently he awarded Fama a few extra banknotes and kola-nuts, in compensation. Fama refused, of course; he had fought for honour alone. No one believed him ... The elder insisted, Fama gave in and pocketed what he'd been given, but remained preoccupied with how degenerate the Malinke had become, how depraved their customs. The dead man's shade would inform the ancestors that under the suns of Independence, Malinke insulted their prince and even went so far as to strike him. Shades of the ancestors! Shades of Moriba, founder of the dynasty! Truly it was time, high time to mourn the sorry fate of the last legitimate Dumbuya!

The ceremony continued. Some gave, others received; all praised the dead man, said how pious he was, how humane, how hospitable. A neighbour even recalled how one night the deceased had brought him a woman's cloth and pair of drawers: they belonged to his (the neighbour's) wife, and the wind had blown them under the deceased's bed. The effect was instantaneous: people's faces relaxed, they burst out laughing. Fama alone did not laugh. Even with the banknotes in his pocket, and in his heart the honour of having been in the right, he was still consumed with anger.

Damn all the bastards! He! Fama, the descendant of the Dumbuya! had been scorned, provoked, insulted, and by whom? The son of a slave. He turned his head. Bamba's mouth was working, his eyes were rolling, his nostrils flared like a horse's after a gallop. He was sturdy, his limbs like stout well-rounded pestles, and Fama wondered if he weren't perhaps too old to challenge him to a wrestling-match.

But he, Fama still clung to the good old ways: a man should never be without a weapon. He felt his pocket; the knife was there, long enough to spill the guts of that son of a dog. Just let Bamba try again, he'll soon find out that however toothless the hyena, its mouth will never make a path for the goat to stroll through.

There were bursts of laughter. Fama pricked up his ears. He had been right not to calm down, not to forgive; that son of a donkey of a praise-singer was intermingling his praise of the deceased with venomous innuendoes: what was the connection between the deceased, and descendants of great warrior families who were prostituting themselves through beggary, quarrels and dishonour? He's no son of a caste, he's a son of a dog! The real praise-singers, the last of the true caste of praise-singers, were buried with Samory's great war captains. This squawker here didn't know how to sing, or talk, or listen. And the man kept going; he even walked about a bit until he was standing behind a pillar. For one of his shameless kind, a pillar is as good a barrier as a river or a mountain. Standing there, he let himself go, and went too far: descendants of great warriors (that was Fama!) were living off lies and beggary (that was still Fama), authentic descendants of great chiefs (Fama again) had traded their dignity for a vulture's plumage, and were forever scenting out new events, a birth, a marriage, a death, so as to hop from one ceremony to another. Fama gathered up his robe in order to rise and reply, but hesitated. This delay encouraged the damned praise-singer, who launched into the grossest of insults with as much delight as a Bambara leaping into the dance-circle at the sound of drums.

No, really! Fama rose and interrupted:

'Fellow-Muslims! One word, fellow-Muslims! Listen ...'

He was not able to utter another word. Like a pack of rutting dogs, all those damned Malinke sitting there, those so-called Muslims, began to howl, bared their fangs and barked insults. Things had gone too far.

Diminished by shame and dishonour, how could he stay? No regrets, either: the ceremony had degenerated into a pack of baboons at play. Best leave the apes to their snapping and tail-pulling. He hurried out. Two men ran to stop him. He struggled free, called them both bastard sons of dogs, and left.

This spectacular exit was greeted only with amused laughter and sighs of relief. Fama would be present next time, and at all Malinke ceremonies in the capital city; everyone knew it. Who ever saw the hyena stop hanging about the graveyard, or the vulture, the refuse-pit behind the village? Everyone knew, too, that Fama would behave badly and give rise to further scandal. In what company does the mastiff ever change his shameless way of sitting? ...

2 *Without the scent of green guava*

Out on the street, Fama stormed, muttered and fumed; his anger died down by not one little ember. He ordered himself to wait for that son of a dog Bamba, and convince all the degenerate bastards that on this earth there still lived a manly man, a man of honour on whom no one could lay a hand with impunity.

The street, one of the busiest of the capital city's African quarter, swarmed with passers-by. On the right, towards the sea, clouds were growing, bringing the horizon nearer the houses. On the left, the peaks of the tall buildings of the European quarter had drawn more clouds to swell that part of the sky. Another storm! The bridge stretched over a lagoon of laterite soil deposited by the week's rains; and the sun, already harried by drifting clouds in the west, had ceased to shine on the African quarter to concentrate on the white buildings of the white men's town. Damnation! Hell! The African is in Hell! The buildings, bridges and roads over there, all built by African hands, were lived in by Europeans and belonged to them. Independence couldn't do a thing about it! Everywhere, under every sun, on every soil, Africans hold the beast's feet, while the Whites carve it up and wolf down the meat and fat. Was it not Hell to toil in the shadows for others? like the giant ant-eater to dig burrows for others? In foul Hell, therefore, all these Africans going up and down the street. In vile and wretched Hell, therefore, the bastard Bamba who had laid a hand on Fama. Then why stand about on the pavement waiting for one of the damned? When a fool shakes his rattle, it should always be another fool who dances; never a descendant of the Dumbuya.

Fama told himself to move on, and crossed the street. There was a little time yet before fourth prayer, time enough to reach the mosque if he walked quickly. Avoiding two taxis, he turned right, skirted a compound and came out on the right-hand pavement of the central avenue, where he joined the crowd flowing towards the market. There, between the roofs, showed a mixture of skies: one tormented by the winds which snatched clouds and flung them at the already overcast and dying sun, and the lower-lying heavy indigo rising from the sea and moving towards the houses and the unquiet trembling trees. The storm was near. Filthy city, sticky with rain, rotten with rain! Ah! the longing for Fama's native land: its deep distant sky, its soil arid but firm, its ever-dry days. Oh! Horodugu, you were what this city lacked, and everything that had given Fama the happy childhood of a prince, that too was lacking (sun, honour and gold): when at rising the slave grooms brought the horse for the morning parade, when at second prayer the praise-singers sang the everlasting power of the Dumbuya, and afterwards the marabouts recited the Koran and taught alms-giving and mercy. Who then could have thought he would come to be hurrying from one ceremony to the next, a beggar?

Memories of childhood, of the sunlit days, the dry harmattan wind, the mornings and smells of Horodugu swept away the offence and drowned his anger. One must be reasonable. God made this life like a cloth of many-coloured strips: one strip the colour of happiness and joy, one strip the colour of poverty and illness, one strip the colour of insult and dishonour. And to be fair, could Fama claim to have been entirely in the right? His heart had not remained cool, his tongue had moved too quickly. A chief's son, a Muslim, should always keep a cool heart and remain patient. Rushing through things at a gallop, we risk burying someone alive; and a hasty tongue can ensnare us in troubles we cannot escape by flight.

There now stirred in the streets and in the leaves of trees the winds that announced rain. The corner of the sky where clouds had been gathering was now swollen to bursting-point, a seething, glinting mass. Fama entered the market-place which lay behind the Senegalese mosque. The market was over, but its smells lingered in spite of the wind. These were the smells of all the great African markets, in Dakar, Bamako, Bobo, Bouaké; the markets Fama had known when he was a big trader. The trader's life was only a memory now; trade died when the colonizers left. What remorse! Fama burned with remorse because he had hated the French and opposed their presence, rather like the blade of grass that complained because the tall tree was taking all the sunlight; once the tree was felled, it had its share of the sun, but also of the wind, which crushed it. Let no one take Fama for a colonialist, mind. For he had seen the colonial era, had known the French administrators who meant many things and many troubles: forced labour in the wood-cutting camps, on the roads and bridges; taxes and more taxes, and fifty other levies such as every conqueror demands, not to forget the lash of the whip and other torments.

But what matters most to a Malinke is freedom of trade. And the French, also and above all, stood for the freedom of trade that enabled the Jula, the big Malinke traders, to prosper. It was through trade and war together that the Malinke race, like one man, heard, saw, walked and breathed; these two things were at once its eyes, its ears, its feet, its loins. The colonial period outlawed and killed war, but favoured trade; Independence ruined trade, and there was no sign of war. So the Malinke species, tribes, land and civilization, was dying: crippled, deaf, blind ... and sterile.

That was why, if he had been free to choose his own poison, Fama would have chosen the colonial period, even though the French had deprived him of his inheritance, and he would have had the blessing of the man who ... Let us briefly recount what happened. When his father died, Fama, his legitimate son, should have succeeded him as chief of all Horodugu. But he came up against intrigues, dishonour, sorcery and lies. In the first place, a little boy, a rascally little European administrator always dressed in dirty shorts, restless and rude as a billy-goat's beard, was put in charge of Horodugu. Of course, Fama could not respect him; that made the man's ears turn red, and he gave the preference to, can you guess? Cousin Lasina, a distant relative who in order to succeed had cast spells, sacrificed beast upon beast, intrigued, lied and crawled so low that ... Men are impatient; but divine justice and the divine will are always done sooner or later. Do you know what happened? Independence and the one-party system disgraced Cousin Lasina, removed him from office and left him worth no more than a vulture's droppings.

After the market, the central avenue led to the cemetery and beyond that to the lagoon, which could be glimpsed at the end under heavy rain. Fama knew this central avenue as well as he knew his wife Salimata's body; it reminded him both of trade and of anti-colonialist activities.

When you came right down to it, though, who among the well-to-do would still remember Fama's efforts? Like a distant storm the suns of Independence had given warning of their coming, and at the first gusts of wind Fama had shed everything: trade, friends, women, to use up his nights and days, his money and his anger in railing against France, the father and mother of France. He wanted revenge for fifty years' domination, and for the loss of his birthright. That period of agitation has been called the suns of politics. After the suns of politics, Independence fell upon Africa like a swarm of grasshoppers. Fama had been like the little swamp rat who digs a hole for the rat-catcher snake; his efforts had brought about his ruin, for like a leaf that's just been used to wipe somebody's arse, once Independence had been won Fama was thrown to the flies and forgotten. That was understandable while they were appointing ministers, deputies, ambassadors; for those, reading and writing is not quite as pointless as rings for a leper. There was an excuse for leaving Fama out of it, since he had remained as illiterate as a donkey's tail. But when Africa discovered, first the one-party system (the one-party system, you know, is like a society of witches, the highest-ranking initiates devour the others' children) and then the co-operatives that ruined trade, there were fifty opportunities to do Fama a favour by making him secretary-general of a party subsection or director of a co-operative. What had he not done to be co-opted? Prayers night and day, all kinds of sacrificial offerings, even a black cat down a well; and it would have been worth it! For the two fattest, meatiest morsels of Independence are undoubtedly the posts of secretary-general and co-operative director ... As long as they are careful to praise the president, the one and only chief, and his party the one and only party, the director and the secretary-general can swallow up all the money in the world, and in all of Africa not one eye will dare blink.

What then did Independence bring Fama? Only the national identity card and the party membership card. These are the poor man's share, dry and hard as bull's meat. Let him tear at them with the fangs of a starving mastiff, he'll get nothing out of them: nothing to chew, nothing to suck, just pure gristle. Since he is too old to go back to the land (the soil of Horodugu is hard, and can only be tilled with strong arms and a back that can stand much bending), all Fama can do is wait for God to provide him with a handful of rice, praying all the while to the merciful Benefactor; for while God is in heaven, even all of them put together, the sons of slaves, the one and only party and the one and only chief, will never succeed in starving him to death.

The rain had moved up the avenue as far as the cemetery. It paused there, blown back by the wind; the sky began to clear over the lagoon, and the cemetery itself became visible. The African cemetery was like the African quarter itself: not enough room. The buried dead had a year in which to rest and rot away; then they dug them up again. A bastard's life for a few months' rest: let's say it's a bit short! Fama passed two Syrian shops on the right and a third on the left, but with a wry smile made a detour to avoid Abjawdi's. That bastard Abjawdi, when the bottom dropped out of trade, found nothing better to do than set up as a money-lender. Fama fed him promises like rock-salt to a donkey, and went into debt up to his neck and beyond while the Syrian still trusted him. When that trust was shaken, Fama exhorted him to pray God that he, Fama, might contrive to pay him back somehow, for under the harsh suns of Independence, to earn money by an honest day's work is something of a miracle, and miracles belong to God alone, who can tell good from evil.

Fama turned left; there was the Julas' mosque. It swarmed with beggars, cripples and blind men hounded from the bush by famine. Trembling hands reached out to him, but the nasal chanting, the purulent eyes, the severed ears and noses, not to mention the peculiar smells, turned Fama's heart cold. He pushed his way past them as if clearing a path in the bush; stepping over mutilated bodies, he entered the mosque imbued with a strong sense of the greatness of God. Peace and confidence flowed through him. With easy royal stride he reached the stairs and climbed the minaret; at the top he paused, then with all his strength, at the top of his voice, proclaimed the call to prayer. He repeated it several times; the day had been a good one, there was something in his pocket and those wretches like ants down below, and at the thought of this his heart suddenly lifted with pleasure, and he stood on tiptoe to call out still louder and to see more.

Over by the lagoon the leprous, greyish tin roofs of the African quarter rippled under a soiled and clammy sky. On the seaward side the rain was being blown back inland, thundering like a herd of buffalo. The first drops rattled and burst against the minaret, and Fama went down into the mosque. A wayward gust of wind struck the wall, rushing through the openings with an angry whistle. The beggars, huddled in a corner, began to panic; their ungodly wailing brought on the storm. Thunder and lightning split the heavens, set fire to the universe, and shook the earth and the mosque with it.

Then, as if bursting free from months of restraint, the sky released torrents of rain which flooded the gutterless streets. The streets had no gutters, because there again Independence had played false, they never dug the gutters they promised and they never will; water will swamp the streets as always, and colonized or independent, the Africans will keep on wading through them until such times as God unpeels the curse stuck fast in their black backsides. Bastards, sons of dogs! Forgive! may God in his mercy forgive Fama for letting such unseemly insults escape him in the mosque!

Fama controlled himself, closed his ears to the roar of storm and flood and his mind to irritating thoughts of Africans bastard and damned, and surrendered himself wholly to prayer. Four times he bowed, knelt, struck the ground with his forehead, rose, then sat cross-legged.

The prayer was in two halves like a kola-nut; the first, a plea for salvation, was recited in Arabic, the language consecrated by God. The second was spoken in Malinke, because it dealt with material things: giving thanks for sustenance, for health, for having eluded the bad luck and evil spells that scorch the black man blacker under the suns of Independence; asking for a mind and heart free of cares and temptations, and filled with peace today, tomorrow and always. Health and sustenance, those Fama had (praise be to God!), but his heart and spirit were heavy and lacked true peace, mainly because of his wife Salimata. Salimata! He clicked his tongue. Salimata, a woman abounding in goodness of heart, in sweet nights and caresses, a true turtle-dove; buttocks low-slung and rounded, back, breasts, hips and belly smooth and infinite to the touch, and always a scent of green guava. May God forgive Fama for evoking Salimata's charms too warmly; the point was that Fama's heart and mind will never know peace, so long as Salimata remains dry and sterile, so long as no child springs up. God! Let her, let Salimata conceive! ... Outside, the rain still fell, the lightning still flashed; inside, the beggars still huddled together, swearing.

Why did Salimata remain sterile? What curse dogged her? She always behaved as a Muslim woman should, performed the proper ablutions, fasted the full thirty days, gave alms and prayed five times daily; Fama could testify to that. And she had tried everything possible: magic spells, marabouts, medicines, sacrificial offerings. But her belly remained as arid as granite; penetrate as deep as you could, dig and delve with the longest and strongest of tools, deposit a handful of selected seed – it all drowned in a great river. Nothing would come of it. The barren, saving divine grace and mercy, never bear fruit.

A flash of yellow lightning lit up the rain and the mosque. The beggars uttered curses and cries of fear, clinging to the walls like little monkeys. They were right. An infernal din crashed down from the sky and rocked the earth. Fama, petrified, broke off his prayer to cry out 'God have mercy on us!' and to cover his head with both hands. The thunder grew weaker, then moved off and died away in the distance. Fama breathed a loud '*Bissimilahi!*' and had to start his prayer over at the beginning. The beggars revived. The rain continued until late. A recluse in God's dwelling-place, Fama prayed fervently several times over, repeatedly asking God for help. Darkness rose from the earth and made the rain seem heavier; lights were turned on. Night had come, and with nightfall Fama's prayers turned once more to Salimata.

Fama felt a pulse of unease within him. Who could reassure him as to the religious purity of Salimata's doings? Trembling limbs, convulsions, amulets and clouds of smoke, all this performance every evening, to make her belly fruitful!

At prayer she recited long and pious verses, like a marabout asking God to turn his stools to gold. But when she had finished, she feverishly brought out amulets, jars, calabashes and herbs, swallowed brews that must be bitter to judge by the way her face twisted in ugly grimaces, burned herbs that filled the room with foul-smelling smoke (Fama hid his face under the bed-cover), and stood over the flames so that the smoke rose under her cloth, penetrating that which cannot be mentioned in a mosque, call it her little pepper-pot, salt-pot, honey-pot, and dispelling (that was Fama's main objection) the intoxicating scent of green guava. Still feverishly, Salimata would dip two fingers in a calabash, smear her breasts, her knees and under her cloth; she hunted out four amulets she fastened to the four bedposts, and the dance began ... To start with, she stamped out a steady rhythm; the ground shook as she jumped and clapped, chanting verses half-Malinke, half-Arabic. But first her limbs, then her whole body began to tremble; her voice faltered, the chanting broke down into sighs, and she collapsed semi-conscious on the mat, like a clinging vine torn from its prop. A moment later, just time enough to lash out with her feet and howl like a demon, she was up again. Breathless, sweaty, smoky and delirious, she flung herself upon Fama and clutched him fast. Weary, yawning and half-asleep though he might be, limp and cold in the lower belly and convinced that there was no point in it with a sterile woman, Fama was expected to perform on the spot and partake of a hot, sticky Salimata, quite devoid of the alluring scent of green guava. Otherwise, beware one of Salimata's dreadful fits of rage! She would rave, scratch and tear, screaming 'You're the one who's sterile, worthless, impotent!'; she would weep all night, and half the morning too. But God and his prophet, you who made us know that there is no drug, no prayer that can turn an empty carcass like Fama into a randy youth, night after night ...

Sin and blasphemy! Fama, did you not know you were sinning in God's dwelling-place? What desecration, to fill your heart and mind with thoughts of Salimata while sitting on a prayer mat in the middle of a mosque! Fama trembled as he realized how greatly he had erred. He began to repent, in order to reconcile himself with God. He had gone too far. A mere hint of Salimata's misdeeds would have been enough; further details were not only sacrilegious, but superfluous and indecent, like dropping your trousers to display a boil when you've merely been asked why you're limping. Merciful God, and Mohammed his prophet! mercy, and again mercy! Fama needed to pray, to ward off thoughts of a life like a rainy afternoon; a life that was dying out amidst poverty and barrenness, Independence and the one-party system! Was not that life like a dead and darkened sun, extinguished in mid-course? The night droned on in a drizzle of rain.

3 *His neck was hung about with collars bristling with magic charms, like the spike-studded collars worn by baboon-hunting dogs*

That night, the frenzied ritual failed to revive Fama; even fear of Salimata's anger could not rouse him, he was tired, truly worn out, and he sank into sleep like a stone into a quiet pool. Then began for Salimata a long night bristling with bitterness. She fanned burning bitter thoughts that dried up sleep and filled the bed with nightmares; she wept and groaned as if some torturer had speared her with a harpoon and were twisting it in the wound.

That night was followed by an evil sun that gave her no respite, a day of misfortune during which her eyes were fixed on her fate, her ears alert to her thoughts; when that day was done she understood God's will and acknowledged her fate. She was destined to be a woman as barren as the dry harmattan wind, as barren as ashes. That was her curse, her misfortune! God alone ordains a creature's destiny.

She began that day by waking too early after her restless night. She tossed and turned in bed, morning was still far off, the paraffin lamp was hissing and its flame flickering, and strewn here and there, on and under the little table, even in the corner of the room, lay the charms, her innumerable magic charms. In order to become fruitful, Salimata had whirled and rattled them, in vain. Fama had not risen, had not been roused. The scattered charms, all warmth and mystery gone, cluttered the room: bottles, salves, jars, ram's horns and amulets. Salimata stroked her abdomen. A meagre belly, covering only entrails and excrement. She pulled back the bedcover and listened. Outside, the cocks were not yet proclaiming morning and sunrise. She closed her eyes, buried her face in the mattress, rolled over and lay against Fama. Fama's snores shook the bed; he was grunting like a boar and lay like a fallen tree-trunk, blocking off most of the bed with his arms and knees. A shameless husband! Irritated, Salimata prodded his ribs with her elbow, but he slumbered on. Nothing worried him, nothing kept him from sleeping, neither impotence nor Salimata's tears nor his failure to perform his conjugal duties. A slight tickling feeling rose in Salimata's throat. She breathed out, breathed in a mouthful of disagreeably damp air, coughed and spat it out. The saliva had an aftertaste of baobab. She pulled the bed-cover over her head. In the morning she would have to be up and about! Like every morning! this would not be the day when Salimata would say to herself, at last I'm pregnant! Her head pounded as if beaten, humming with memories. Excision! its scenes, colours, smells. And rape! its own colours, pain, revulsion.

Rape! Amidst the blood and pain of excision, something had seared her like fiery pepper, like red-hot iron. She had screamed, howled. Her eyes had spun round, spilled over and plunged into the green of the forest, the yellow of the harmattan wind, then red, blood-red, the red of sacrifice. And she had screamed again, screamed as loudly as possible, with all her strength; screamed until she choked and fainted. She did not know how long she had remained unconscious. When her senses revived, people were standing murmuring above her, the paraffin lamp was blazing brightly, her thighs were wet with blood and the mat was soaked with it; she had started to bleed again as she had bled the previous morning; her mother could not stop weeping and wailing. Poor mother!... Poor mother!...

Just then, a bedbug bit Salimata on the buttock; she chased it as far as Fama's feet and shoulders, captured it near the pillow and crushed it. A stench of excrement stuck between her fingers. Nasty creature! She pushed back the bed-cover; she was too hot. Fama's snores filled the room. Her thoughts turned once more to the excision, her pain, her disappointment, and her mother...

Poor mother! how she had suffered, many times over, for her daughter's sake! Especially on the dramatic occasion of her daughter's initiation ceremony! She had always imagined how her daughter would return, beautiful and brave, from the field of excision, decked with a hundred ornaments, dancing and singing while she, her mother, cried out with pride.

'You'll see,' she would often say when Salimata was a very little girl, 'you'll see, one day you'll be initiated. It's not just a celebration, with dancing, singing and feasting; it's also something very important, an event with a deep meaning.'

But what was the meaning?

'You'll see, my daughter: for a month you'll lead a life apart, along with the other initiated girls, and along with the singing they'll teach you all the taboos of our tribe. Initiation is a turning-point, a break with the years of equivocal, impure girlhood, the beginning of your life as a woman.'

When Salimata's breasts sprouted and hardened, her mother exclaimed with joy:

'Ah! you're a grown girl now! it won't be long.'

And in the middle of one rainy season:

'The day has been set, it will be during the coming harmattan season.'

The day ordained duly arrived, one morning during the final week of the dry season, a dull greyish morning like any other, except for the burning ache in Salimata's heart, her mother's anxiety and painful forebodings. At first cock's crow a drum summoned the girls who were to be initiated.

'Be brave, my daughter! Bravery in the field of excision is a mother's pride, and the whole tribe's. I thank God that this morning has come. But I am afraid, my heart is leaping with fear, and I beg all the spirits that the field may be auspicious to my only daughter.'

Yes, the spirits heard her mother's prayer, but how! after what sorrow! after what worries! after what tears!

Salimata would never forget how the girls gathered in the night and walked single file through the forest and the dew; the stream they forded, the shrill singing of the matrons leading them; their arrival at a cleared and tilled field, at the foot of a hill with its wooded summit lost in mist, and the matrons' savage cry proclaiming this to be 'the field of excision'. The field of excision! Salimata's thoughts were interrupted by Fama lashing out; a bedbug must have bitten him. He unbent like a bow, kicking Salimata hard, then resumed his snoring. The blow quickened her anger. It was for that ne'er-do-well, that worthless piece of rubbish empty night and day, that she wore herself out, rising at first cock's crow to cook and sell porridge to earn the money to clothe and feed and house him, then at noon rushing to sell rice at the market to earn money for all the charms, medicines, marabouts and sacrifices required to promote virility and fruitfulness ... And then at night to receive nothing but kicks from a donkey. No! She slapped him hard across the buttocks. Fama grunted but continued to snore, and Salimata once more took up her thoughts.

... They had arrived at the field of excision. She remembered how each girl in turn had unwound and cast aside her cloth, and sat on a upturned earthen jar; then the blacksmith's wife, a powerful sorceress, who was to perform the operation, had brought forth the knife, a knife with a curved blade, displayed it to the surrounding hills, then severed the clitoris that represented impurity, confusion, imperfection; and the girl she had just operated on would rise, thank her, and intone the hymn to glory and courage, all those present taking up the chorus. Salimata could still hear the echoes, amplified by the hills and forest, that had made birds take flight from the trees and baboons begin to bark. She remembered how her belly had rumbled with a rising fear, because of all the tales of girls who had died in the field. Their names had come to mind, the names of those who had fallen under the knife. The field took only the most peerless beauties (like Salimata!). Mussogbe of her mother's age-group had fallen, a beauty all Horodugu still remembered. Four harmattan seasons ago Nuna had not come back, whose nose was as straight as a taut thread. Salimata had looked in vain for their graves: the graves of those who had not returned and had not been mourned, because it was believed that they had died as a sacrifice to ensure the village's future happiness. The forest had swallowed up their burial-place. Salimata could remember how the woman had approached her, when her turn had come. The clamour of the matrons and the girls who'd already come through, the cries of the birds of prey, the echoes from hills and forest had rung loud in her ears. The sun was rising, glowing red behind the leaves. Vultures had come flapping out of the mist and the trees, drawn by the scent of blood. They circled overhead with wild cries. The woman had approached Salimata and squatted, her eyes red-rimmed, her hands and arms hideous with blood, her breath hissing like a waterfall. Salimata had surrendered herself, eyes shut, and the pain had flooded up from between her legs to her back, her neck, her head, and back down to her knees. She had wanted to rise and sing, but could not, her breath failed her, the burning pain stiffened her limbs, the earth seemed to end beneath her feet, and all those present, the matrons and the other girls, the hills and forest seemed to topple over and float away in the misty dawn; a great weight dragged at her eyelids and knees, and she broke and collapsed lifeless to the ground...

How hot, stifling, burning almost like red pepper, was the atmosphere of the room! And Fama's irritating snores. Salimata rose, wrapped her cloth more closely about her, and pushed open the door to see if dawn had yet lit the sky. She was met by the cool night, a rustle of city sounds, a quickening breeze from the sea. There was a dog barking in the distance, and still further off the dull roar of a car passing, unless it were the sound of the waves; the beam of the lighthouse swept over roofs and clumps of trees. A stiffer breeze began to blow, rattling the tin roofs and whistling in the doorway, and brushing Salimata's cheek until she felt sleepy. She closed the door and lay down again, to sleep what little was left of the night.

When Salimata had woken in the field of excision, the sun was high overhead, and there were two matrons by her side. The procession had set out long before. So the return of the initiates had been celebrated, danced and sung without Salimata. Ah! The return, it must be said, was the best part of the whole ceremony, with drumming, singing, rejoicing, and the whole village rushing to meet the returning girls shaking their calabash tambourines. Salimata had not experienced that triumphant return to the village of which she had so often dreamed. She had been carried back in secret on a matron's back, by a disused path and a hidden gate, to the hut of the fetish-priest Chekura, there to lie under the protection of Chekura's fetish. For the rest of the day, sacrifices burned and red and white kola-nuts rolled at her feet, while her mother wept. Salimata had spent the night there; a night she would never forget.

It was a small, round, isolated hut, untidy and swarming with lizards. Inside, the paramount fetish was a hideous mask that took up over half the space; a paraffin lamp shed only a faint smoky glow, so as to preserve the mystery. The thatched roof, old and blackened with smoke, was laden with a thousand trophies: cloths, a basket, a knife and so on. A hanging mat covered the door, also very small, that opened on to the night, the bush, mystery. It was there, just when her eyes had become heavy with sleep, that the mat had been lifted and something had weighed heavily on her hips, something had struck her wound, the pain had pierced and seared her through, her eyes had filmed over with a whirl of flashing colours, green, then yellow, then red, and she had screamed with pain and fainted amidst the red of blood. She had been raped. By whom? A spirit, they said afterwards. They also explained why. Salimata's mother had suffered from sterility, and had been cured only when she prayed to Mount Tugbe, the spirit of which had made her pregnant with Salimata. Salimata was born beautiful, so beautiful as to inspire the love and provoke the jealousy of the spirit, that began to haunt her. She had been promised in marriage, she had been initiated without giving the spirit due warning or soothing its passion by special worship. It was the spirit's jealousy and anger that had provoked the haemorrhage. It was the spirit, in human form, that had tried to rape her in the blood of the wound.

A cock crowed in the next-door compound, the first cry of the day being born. Salimata rushed out, holding the lamp; she built up wood on the hearth of the cook-hut next door, and lit a match; the smoke hissed and made her cough before releasing a singing blue flame. She drew two pails of water from the well in the middle of the compound, poured them into the pot set over the flickering flame, and sat on a stool, her elbows on her knees and her hands under her chin; the heat of the fire was like a murmuring caress from Fama during a cold harmattan night.

But Salimata did not know; she would never know for sure. She did not know if it were really the spirit that had raped her. She had seen the shadow of a man, a figure like the fetish-priest Chekura. She was lying in the fetish-priest's hut; all day long he had roamed about outside the hut, 'to keep the dogs away'. At night he had returned, had greeted Salimata and the matron in attendance. It was after the matron had fallen asleep, and weariness had closed Salimata's eyes, that someone had blown out the lamp and assaulted her wounded body; the figure had trampled her legs, then escaped through the doorway when Salimata screamed. Salimata was not sure, but she thought it might have been the fetish-priest Chekura who had raped her in the wound of excision. Disgust filled her mouth with salty saliva. She spat in to the flames.

No, she would never know for sure, but it had left deep within her a terror that paralysed her whenever anything reminded her of Chekura. For Salimata, Chekura the fetish-priest remained more than a totem! a nightmare, an affliction. Indeed, even without a memory of rape, Chekura was a truly frightening creature, hideous and savage. He had glaring eyes like a black savanna buffalo. His plaited hair, laden with amulets, was haunted by a cloud of flies.

He wore copper earrings, and his neck was welded to his shoulders by iron collars studded with magic charms, like those worn by baboon-hunting dogs. His nose was broad and flat, with a deep eroded furrow between nostril and cheek, like those that form at the foot of hills. He had broad shoulders like a chimpanzee, a hairy chest and limbs; a mouth always pursed in ill-temper, an abrupt way of speaking, a shambling gait and bow-legs. He was the son and grandson of a fetish-priest, born and bred amidst sacrifices and ritual; rainy season and dry, there hung over him the scent of slaughter and burnt offerings, silent mysteries and hidden suffering. This man's silhouette, his shadow, his smell would strike Salimata even from afar with nausea and terror.

No one could see that, no one understood when Salimata refused to give herself to Baffi (her first husband). Baffi stank like a stale warmed-up version of Chekura with the same shambling hyena gait, the same red eyes like a weaver-bird, the same voice, the same breath; his presence petrified her. At the end of the period of retreat following excision (after the night of the rape, Salimata had joined the other initiates in a special hut, and had spent three weeks cloistered with her age-mates, recovering, celebrating and learning the lore of initiation), a young Malinke girl is given in marriage. One evening, Salimata, shivering with fear, was led to her betrothed amidst drumming and singing. The yellow moon stared out from among the clouds, village and forest vibrated with the wedding festivities; her mother trembled and wept, and Salimata could see and hear nothing, she was too frightened. The ceremony was over too soon for her; all too quickly her head was washed, and she found herself in the nuptial room, with two matrons at the foot of the bed to instruct her in sexual matters and bear witness to her virginity. Baffi came in, approached her, made an attempt; her limbs contracted, and she curled up tight in refusal; the matrons rushed to hold her down and he tried to force and rape her; she screamed! She screamed as she had screamed the night after the excision, as all her terrified fear of Chekura rose in her throat; she must have screamed very loudly, for all the dogs began to bark, from one compound to another, frightening the whole village; the matrons let go, she leapt up from the bed to escape through the door, they stopped her, she collapsed in the doorway and lay there weeping bitterly. The husband pulled his trousers back on: Salimata did not even notice that Baffi bulged with a large hernia that gave him the same ground-squirrel gait as Chekura. Advice from the elders and old women, her mother's reassurance and even threats, did nothing to relieve her terror. They tried another wedding night, many more wedding nights, in vain. He would mount her, and she would scream and clutch his strangulated hernia. They realized that they would have to give up the attempt, or she might kill him. Besides, it was useless, quite useless, she belonged to the devil, she was still haunted by the spirit that had raped her; the spirit would not allow Salimata to mate with a man, hence her screams, her horrified refusal, her murderous acts (clutching the hernia). However, since bridewealth had been paid and the marriage duly celebrated, Salimata would continue to live in her husband's compound, as a woman performing her share of the cooking and farming, but not as a wife with a share of her husband's nights, without hope, therefore, of a child. Praise be to God, Lord of the universe, merciful provider! The strangulated hernia did for its man, who collapsed and died. Four years of unconsummated marriage! Salimata spent three months cloistered in her widow's hut.

The pot was humming; Salimata lifted the lamp, the hot water was bubbling, she filled a pail and carried it behind the hut. Fama sprawled snoring, his nose buried in the covers, useless and empty as always, with no compassion for his wife's mad desire for a big belly. She shook him, he turned over and sank once more into a deep sleep. Annoyed, she took aim and with her open right hand slapped once, the left buttock of a husband who did not perform his duties, twice, the right buttock of a ne'er-do-well who knew only how to sleep, and once more, hard, the right buttock of a big eater who brought nothing home.

'Yes! yes! stop hitting me, you bad woman!'

'Get up! or you'll miss first prayer, it's light everywhere outside.'

Then she went to put the pot of porridge on the fire, poured herself a pailful of warm water and bathed. The soothing warmth gave her strength, and the soapy water smelled of morning, of the season, of memories...

... There had been bad, wicked talk against Salimata, during and after her period of reclusion as a widow. People said it wasn't the strangulated hernia that killed Baffi, that he'd been murdered by the jealous evil spirit that haunted Salimata; it was her fault. People pointed her out when telling the story:

'A curse on the beauty that attracts spirits! a woman without a hole! a statue!' and Baffi's brother, who had inherited Salimata, was at first reluctant to introduce into his compound such an ill-omened woman.

'The jealous evil spirit must first be sent away.'

Salimata, alone with her sorrows, alone in her room, in the compound, in the village, night and day for weeks, months, rainy season and dry, heard only the sound of her own weeping. Then, one Monday afternoon, Baffi's brother (his name was Chemoko) came to Salimata. The evil spirit had been exorcized, and he wanted her, he was mad for her, and jealous. He pulled a knife:

'You'll lie with me, or else ...' and he flourished the knife.

Except for the hernia, Chemoko was as like his brother Baffi, and therefore Chekura, as two footprints of a single beast. He was even more frightening than Baffi: his eyes blazing with violence, abnormally alert and quick to take offence like all people who spend their time in the bush (he was a hunter by profession), opening his mouth only to utter insults and threats, and forever brandishing a knife or gun. When love and jealousy appeared in his mouth and his red eyes, no good could come of it, for Salimata froze when he drew near, and the excision, rape, Chekura and misery all swept over her again. She told him so. He responded by shutting her up in a hut about which he circled night and day, knife and gun at the ready, hurling threats and insults at his captive, at all liars and people of evil counsel, and the accursed era of European rule, that wouldn't let a man cut the throat of a damned adulteress.

One night she had escaped and run alone through the bush alone in the dark...

She rinsed herself, and there remained only to pour over her head the contents of the pail of warm water; she did so, and still wet, wrapped herself in her cloth. In the hut, she pulled out the goatskin, unfolded it, and began the good, comforting morning prayer. Four times she rose and touched her forehead to the ground, then she sat on the goatskin and confided in God, the merciful provider. A child! Just one! Yes, a baby! That was the one thing on earth she prayed for, as Fama proved more and more inadequate. What stood foremost in God's will? Fidelity or motherhood? Motherhood surely, motherhood above all. Then let Fama's image fade from Salimata's heart, let her be able to lie with other men who would no longer evoke the features and smells of the fetish-priest Chekura, other men who would no longer make Salimata's body stiffen and turn cold with fear. But she was praying that she might

27

be unfaithful, commit adultery. God, merciful provider, forgive the blasphemy! Had she sinned? No! Salimata was not an impious sinner; her marriage bound together a sterile husband and a faithful wife, she was imploring God, the all-forgiving, the merciful, that motherhood might visit her there. She smiled slightly, but quickly repressed it: never smile while on God's prayer mat.

The darkness of night lingered only in corners, under eaves and among foliage, about to be absorbed into the substance of things. The sky arched higher now. To the east rose four or five glowing slabs of stone, with small clouds drifting past. The city was turning light with morning. Salimata hastily recited the final verses, finished her prayers, folded the goatskin and went outside.

Fama had gone to the mosque, where he said first prayer every morning. The porridge was ready; she set aside a plateful for Fama, well sweetened. Whatever the man's behaviour, whatever he might be worth, a husband was still a sovereign ruler, to whom a wife owed all her care. God has ordained that a woman be submissive in her husband's service; his commandments must be obeyed, for they signify strength, valour, grace and quality for the child of such a wife. And the child, should God grant him, would be a man whose trace on earth would never vanish, not in millions of years. Great men are born of women who have long endured the trouble, the tears, the worries and weariness of marriage...

She emptied the pot into a basin, rushed into the room, wrapped a clean cloth round her, pulled on a blouse, and with the basin on her head went out the back door into the street. Walking on sand still wet with dew, she crossed the market-place (it was still empty) and reached the wharf.

Two long-boats full of passengers were rocking on the grey lagoon, where blew a damp clinging wind. Passengers and boatmen were laughing. The most agile of the boatmen leapt out to un-burden Salimata, helped her into the boat, then handed her the basin. They were leaving straight away, the motor exploded and stuttered, the craft spun round and headed for the open sea and the European quarter glittering on higher ground in the light of dawn.

'Did you spend the night in peace?'

'Peace only, praise be to God. May the Lord's goodness grant us a happy day!'

The woman next to Salimata was a colleague, a friend. Every morning they met at the wharf, every morning they sold plates of porridge to the workers waiting outside shops, workshops and building-sites for the signal that started the working day.

Once they were clear of the shore, the motor's noise seemed to fade and die away, gentled by the cool half-light of the lagoon. The African quarter dwindled in the distance and was lost amidst dark clumps of trees; the European quarter, still faint in the distance, shone with street-lamps. All you could see clearly was the grey lagoon and the multi-coloured sky. On the right, dead-white clouds streaked a blazing backdrop of sky; further to the north-east, a great golden band spanned the horizon as far as the highest point of the European quarter. On the lagoon, bobbing launches cut white trails between the silhouetted long-boats that met, inter-mingled, disappeared. Through the arches of the bridge, you could see the lights of the ships lying asleep in the harbour. A sudden spreading glow! The morning had just won through, the golden clouds clearly took pleasure in crowding out the grey sky. On the high ground across the lagoon, the European quarter was looming larger, aloof and regal with its tall buildings and many-coloured villas set among clumps of mango-trees. A calm, relaxed feeling flooded Salimata: peace of heart. The lagoon wrinkled as if in time to the beat of the motor and the snatches of cha-cha tunes the boat-man was humming. Something about the tone of his voice reminded her of Fama. Salimata turned round; the singer was half-hidden behind a passenger, but what she could see of him confirmed the likeness: not with the empty carcass of a scavenger, but with the young and handsome Fama Salimata had gone to join when she fled the village.

That escape! She had fled alone through the grey night with a bundle clutched under her arm, on a path through the dark bush haunted with spirits and infested with wild beasts. She had run through thorns, across streams, on stones, run bathed in sweat until she almost suffocated. Nothing had stopped her: neither fear of the night, nor of the wild beasts, nor the snakes. Nothing! She had seen, heard, thought of nothing but what she was fleeing, that every breath she took panting with weariness, every hill climbed, every river forded, every forest crossed set further behind her, that was cast off with the gravel that flew beneath her feet in the plains, and silenced by the cries and howls he passed through, the hiss-ing snakes she avoided: excision, rape, sequestration, the knife, weeping, suffering, loneliness, a whole life of misery. At one point she had felt her knees buckle, her heart fail, her eyes grow dim, her back break. She couldn't run any more, and she had stopped, but only for a short time, because at once the bush had come alive. What was that noise? Was it Chemoko? Was she being pursued? On the point of being caught? At that thought her legs shed their weariness, her heart suffocation, her eyes dizziness. She set out again on the path, with new-found strength and her second wind, and ran faster than before. She knew what to expect if she were caught: if her throat were not cut on the spot, she would be dragged back to the village, once more to be locked up at night and guarded during the day by Chemoko, armed and maddened by jealousy. That was what had set her running once more. For some time there had been a glow at the horizon, then suddenly the moon had risen, and the bush had turned pale but remained mysterious. Once more she had collapsed at the foot of a tree, overcome by despair and exhaustion. Panting, she had thought of what was drawing near with the distance travelled and the fear and weariness overcome: Fama, love, a married woman's life, an end to imprisonment. She had remembered the first time she had seen Fama among the dancers: the tallest young man in Horodugu and the darkest, gleaming charcoal-black, with white teeth and the gestures, the voice, the riches of a prince. She had loved him at once, and he, Fama, had sighed:

'Salimata, you are the loveliest living thing in all the bush and villages of Horodugu.'

Since that time, in all her torment and misery, her misfortunes and bitter worries, she had never forgotten him. And he was the one who would be there when the night was over and the race was run, when she could breathe once more. She had risen, and again started to run. The moon had turned white. She had run until morning, until the first town she reached. Chemoko had not caught her that night, he had not even pursued her. When he had found her gone, he had spent the rest of the night searching the village, one hut after another, with a knife in his hand. The next day, his finger poised on the trigger of his gun, he had roamed the bush, the hills and streams. The following days, without eating, drinking or sleeping, he had vented his rage and sorrow throughout the fields and villages of the province.

By then, Salimata was far away and had found her Fama. A Fama still peerless, awakening the desire to touch him, caress him, listen to him, drink him in. The Fama brought to mind by the boatman humming a cha-cha tune...

They had arrived. The wharf at the edge of the European quarter reached out towards them. The motor stopped its drum-beat and began hissing like a trapped civet-cat. The huge sun, blazing like a blacksmith's forge, had climbed high in the sky, and a broad band of copper ran from east to west across the lagoon. The morning was alive and humming with activity: on the wharf, workers who had just landed were hurrying off, boatmen and fishermen were already busy, women hawked their wares. Frightened by the uproar, clouds of bats and weaver-birds rose screeching from the palms and mango-trees clustered about the white buildings.

'Here, boatman! May God grant you health, long life and prosperity.'

The man who had helped Salimata unload her basin felt the coin and slipped it in his pocket, deaf and indifferent to her good wishes.

'Come! Now you must wish me blessings, that the market and the day may be favourable, that I may be fruitful and rich with children like those bats!'

Startled, the boatman automatically repeated the phrases, then walked away.

Salimata went up the Syrians' avenue. On the right was the crowded Niger Company square. Further on, in ragged clothes and broad straw hats, workers from the North were gorging on bread and coffee.

'Porridge! good sweet porridge!' she called out.

A little street between tall red buildings, with flowered balconies and here and there a white woman dandling a round laughing baby, with a proud broad-shouldered husband by her side. Peace and happiness! May God grant Salimata peace and happiness! Then came the building-site at the end of the street, where all Salimata's customers were milling about.

'Porridge! good sweet porridge!'

She was soon surrounded by customers. Just say, 'God grant you a child!' and she'd give you credit. She was a bit crazy with kindness, you might say. Bat's ears, a flattened nose, ritual scars running down to his neck: that was Mussa Wedrago. He owed for between six and ten helpings of porridge, and he'd been out of work for two whole weeks. Were you supposed to let a human being suffer because he hadn't been signed on that day? May God transform the mother's good deeds into strength and good fortune for the child!

'Here, take this helping on credit, Wedrago!'

And honey-tongued Traore had promised the powder that makes most barren woman fruitful.

'One porridge!'

And Mamadawu! He always paid cash. But he was a man she didn't like, a cook on the building-site, who dared to proposition Salimata. In front of everyone. As if she were a chit who sold herself along with the porridge. She wanted to be a mother, a worthy mother; immoral mothers make unlucky children. And motherhood is a great thing, a difficult thing, only to risk ending up with a disobedient creature that brings you only worries, instead of supporting mother and father in their old age.

And Chemoko, Bakary, Cheffy: all received helpings on credit. The basin was empty and clean, and the bell rang to signal the start of work. Salimata would return at noon. The bell rang again. The circle surrounding her broke and scattered. The cement-mixers groaned and thundered. Hammers struck. Other machines roared. The whole building-site rang with noise as if a storm and whirlwind had taken it over.

Plates in the basin and the basin balanced on her head, Salimata walked along the bougainvillea-lined street that led to the wharf, until she reached the roundabout. There, the avenue led to a platform with railings and flights of steps to the right and left. From there the African quarter, the bridge, the whole lagoon spread out to infinity like the songs girls sing at initiation. The sun had reached its full strength and mastery. Long-boats followed the white trails traced by heavy launches. The various neighbourhoods of the African quarter intermingled, as far as the place where there were three or four bright-coloured two-storey houses, then a church and a large cinema. Further on rose among the foliage the white mists of lagoon and forest.

The day was still long: there was the market to visit, the rice to cook and sell, the marabout to visit, and all before third prayer. The sun was already hot overhead, launches were setting out and all the cheaper goods were already being snapped up, those that would bring in enough money to feed Fama, clothe Fama, house Fama, to pay the marabouts and the sorcerers who made magic charms. She tightened her cloth, set the basin straight on her head, went down the steps from the platform, crossed the avenue and the quay, and walked along the left-hand pavement. At the edge of the quay lay heaps of rubbish, their strong clinging stench mingling with the acrid odours of the lagoon. She held her breath, walked along the furrow traced by the bare feet of passers-by, and reached the platform of the quay, loud with the cries of boatmen. A launch was just leaving, and Salimata embarked.

The motor backfired, the craft swung round and cleft the wrinkled surface of the lagoon.

Once clear of the shore, the sole master of all was the sun: its glare, its glitter on the water, its heat. The motor's squawk, damped and stifled by the open space, was almost lost in the deep water.

Once she had escaped from mad Chemoko, and found Fama again to love and live with, days of happiness had begun. Yes, Salimata had lived in happiness for weeks, months and years on end, but unfortunately there was no child. That is what every couple, every woman should have: motherhood and a child are worth more than the richest ornaments, more than the most dazzling beauty. A woman who is not a mother lacks more than half of what makes a woman.

In all her thoughts, feelings, prayers Salimata longed for a child. Her dreams overflowed with baskets crammed with babies, babies everywhere. She bathed them, cradled them, and her sleeping heart was filled with joy, until she woke. In broad daylight, even out in the street, she could sometimes hear babies crying and calling her. She would stop and listen: nothing! It was the wind whistling, or passers-by hailing each other. One morning she was rinsing dishes: her fingers touched a baby, a real baby. She bathed him, he wriggled and cried. She carried him into the room, and opened her eyes. Nothing: a hard brittle ladle, and Salimata standing there in shame and despair. One night in bed, a baby suddenly clung to Salimata and began to suckle, his mouth burned her left breast, then the right. She could feel him, warm and round and soft. She lit the lamp: gone, changed into a mortar from the cook-hut. Who could have put that mortar in the bed? Salimata could guess, and the sorcerers confirmed it; the dire spirit that had haunted her in the village, had joined her in the capital city. It loved Salimata and would not leave her. The result of its attentions soon appeared: the spirit made Salimata pregnant!

What matter that after everything had collapsed and vanished, the doctor had called it a 'hysterical pregnancy' and the Malinke, a 'spirit pregnancy'! Salimata had been happy, exultant, for months and months; she was pregnant, developed a belly and all the other signs of pregnancy. She had gone to the maternity clinic, where she had been examined, pronounced pregnant, and entered on the neighbourhood register of pregnant women.

For months, like all the pregnant women in the neighbourhood, her spoon and health card in hand, Salimata had walked up 5th Street, crossed one to two compounds, then reached 8th Avenue and the big market; she had greeted passers-by, telling them that she was going to the dispensary to take the pregnant women's dose of medicine, and they had promptly congratulated her, heaped blessings upon her for a safe delivery and a child to be proud of, and praised God who had rewarded Salimata's good deeds, her kindness and prayers with the gift of motherhood.

That went on for month after month, then a year, without a birth! Two years. Nothing! Little by little the belly waned, and all the signs of pregnancy dwindled and disappeared. The worst of such things is the shame, afterwards; you wish you could split the earth open and hide in it. After months of pregnancy, with no miscarriage and no birth, you have to go out and about like other people, see other people and talk to them, laugh and joke with them. When you talk to people, you can tell they're choking back questions. Each time you become something – something different, afraid of everyone...

The boat let out an angry wheeze. They had arrived. Salimata walked up to the market.

The market! First a dull humming that penetrated your whole body and made it vibrate, and the wind heavy with foul smells. Then a row of bougainvillea, and the market with its swarming throng and the din of a thousand different voices. Everything wriggled and whirled as if dancing to festive drums, the cars squealing round a corner, the vendors shouting themselves hoarse and gesturing as if wielding slingshots. Deaf to their cries, the housewives appealed to went calmly to and fro, examining one stall after another. The roofs of the stalls, all interlinked, echoed, channelled and amplified this beehive noise, so that you felt closed in, as though someone had trapped you under a calabash like a chick, and were drumming on it. Salimata crossed the market, past the vegetable stalls with their lettuces, cabbages, radishes giving off a cool scent of dew, then the fruit stalls. She lingered there. A little boy of eighteen months old was toddling about naked as a needle, his nose and eyes filthy with snot and swarming with flies, and held his arms out to Salimata. A child! to have a child, and neglect it so! It's always those whose earlobes aren't strong enough for heavy earrings, who find gold. The little boy tripped over the curled-up corner of a mat, and fell on his face in the sand. Salimata hurried to pick him up.

'May God reward you with a child!' exclaimed the mother.

'May he hear and grant your good wishes.'

Then there were the women selling dried fish and fresh, with the lingering smells of bush-fires, dried-up ponds, sea vapours and lagoon stench; then the circle of women selling rice. She had come to buy the rice to cook for midday, and paid for five measures. More stalls, more vendors, always the same noise and smells, and she had crossed the market. The south gate of the covered area gave on to the street where Salimata's compound was. The neighbourhood was alive with noise and bustle.

Salimata entered the compound through the front door. In the middle of the courtyard, under mango-trees swarming with weaver-birds, amidst scattered calabashes, children and chickens, some women were pounding grain. They had spent a peaceful night, was their response to Salimata's greetings, along with loud bursts of laughter. Fama was sitting in the room, useless and empty at night, useless and empty in the daytime, a weary worn-out thing like an old chipped calabash. Yet the look of him was still pleasing: tall as a silk-cotton tree, with shoulders, arms and face still likely to win an oh! of admiration from a woman who didn't know him.

'Salimata, did you do well at the market?'

As if deaf, she busied herself with household tasks, tidied utensils, changed into one of the cloths she wore for cooking, carried a pot outside. The pestle beat out a rapid rhythm. She returned carrying a basin. Still he waited for an answer to his greeting.

'Yes, I did well at the market. What about you? Tell me! Are you going to spend the whole long day like that, sprawling on a chair?'

Fama in turn feigned indifference, and did not answer; he appeared to be busy counting the curses brought by the suns of Independence. Salimata hadn't the time, the day was already far gone and there was too much left to do. The rice was in the pot, boiling even, but she would have to keep an eye on it, and there was the sauce still to prepare.

She moved a small mortar nearer the fire, and began to pound the condiments. The pestle beat as loudly as a drum announcing bad news, so she did not have to hear, see or sense the presence of Fama thus gone stale. How far away they were, the months when she was expecting a child! The pestle kept on pounding. Consumed, reduced to ashes the love that Fama and Salimata had had for each other then!

She had loved him enough to swallow him whole! A hard-working trader, he was often away; she waited for him, spent days and nights thinking of the sound of his footsteps, the tone of his voice, the creak of his stiffly-starched robe.

He would return, and every time there would be something more to his smile, his white teeth, his warm heart. He stayed that way, ever-dazzling, ever-thoughtful, until her belly waned!

Afterwards, their household knew neither the repose of peace nor the remote sweetness of happiness. Fama became resigned to the idea that Salimata was incurably sterile. He sought out fruitful women, even tried (oh! the shame) some of the capital city's women of easy virtue. First one, then a second, then a third. Nothing came of it. All of them lasted for months at a stretch, sometimes spoke of marriage, but as one season shaded into another they remained empty and dry, like ears of millet when the rains have ended too soon, then they left. Indeed, how could they have stayed? Misfortune was now Fama's constant companion; misfortune took part in everything he undertook, guided his every gesture as he went about his business. Bargains, purchases, sales, journeys all ended in failure. Only despair remained. Pride, warmth, kindness vanished. Fama was a changed man. It was then that politics came on the scene. Fama dropped everything to throw himself into politics, with much eloquence and bravery. A legitimate son of chiefs must devote himself wholly to the task of expelling the French. In politics there was room for manliness and revenge, and there were nearly fifty years of occupation by the infidels to denounce, challenge, undo.

Salimata's thoughts were interrupted by a hissing noise from the fire. Froth from the boiling rice had overflowed and extinguished the flames.

She put down the pestle and bent over the hearth: the rice was cooked. The sauce was simmering, and she sprinkled in the contents of the mortar, salt and red pepper. She put rice on a plate and sauce in a bowl, then kneeling laid them at Fama's feet. The husband was served.

'Thank you for your cooking, may God reward you for it!'

She went back into the stifling cook-hut, grey with smoke that stung her eyes, nose and throat, scattered the embers and carried the cooking-pots into the courtyard; then she too sat down, swallowed handfuls of rice, bit into pieces of meat. The meat was tough, but the sauce was very good; the rice was a bit underdone. She gathered up her things, the sun was moving fast and the bell would soon ring for midday break over the European quarter. After washing quickly, she changed cloths, settled the basins on her head, and picked up her stool:

'I'm going to the white men's town, to the place where they sell rice.'

'May God grant you good fortune and a favourable market,' replied Fama, busy washing his hands over the empty dishes.

4 *When has God ever shown pity for misfortune?*

It was noon, between seasons. God himself had left his heaven to take refuge in a quiet corner of his vast world, leaving the sun up there to invade and occupy the sky as far as the horizon. The earth was shimmering with mirages. Streets and quays clanged and glittered from afar amid showers of sparks. At the wharf boats were arriving and departing, making the crossing quickly in spite of the heat and the light reverberating from the lagoon, and Salimata soon found herself on the quay of the European quarter, her body and breath already adjusted to the heat, and her eyes to the mirages.

The cooked-rice market was just a few paces from the wharf. Other women had already set out their wares in the shelter of their stalls. Among the vendors, around the stalls loitered the unemployed, and files of beggars roamed about: blind, crippled, crazy. The paying customers hadn't arrived yet, the noon break hadn't sounded, but it wouldn't be long now.

Salimata sat down in an inconspicuous place, with no stall, table or bench; she did just as well as the others, for God rewards goodness of heart; good temper and good humour are the most important things, and if you're cut of Salimata's cloth, there's no problem, customers will come even if you settle on an anthill.

The other women at their stalls were jealous of her, and gossiped maliciously. Look at Salimata selling her rice out there in the sun! Badly cooked rice, too! And on credit! With her hypocritical smiles! They said all that, and more. Truly they were unworthy to be mothers; with such wicked hearts, they could cut a chicken's throat over a white cloth and not leave a single stain. God, you who weigh good and evil, how could you justify having given these unkind creatures offspring, while Salimata, a true Muslim ...

But noon had just sounded on the building-sites and in the

offices. The hungry workers jostled each other at the gates, poured into the open spaces, the streets, cars and boats.

'Good cooked rice! Very cheap! Come buy good cooked rice!'

Packs, swarms of men crowded into the little market-place. Serried ranks of plate-bearing hands crossed under Salimata's eyes and nose. Quick as the feet of a deer her hands moved to and fro, filling plates with rice, spooning on sauce with a piece of meat on top, taking payment (fifteen francs) and tucking the money into her cloth. She smiled briefly to right and left in response to greetings:

'Peace only!'

'May God give you good fortune, a lucky market and many children!'

'May he hear you!'

As deft and agile as a weaver's, her hands darted from plate to pail of rice to red sauce, and tucked more and more money into the corner of her cloth. The heavenly provider had made trade prosper. Thanks be to God! The little market was at its peak of activity, the din spread from the stalls to the wharf and even to the lagoon, where long-boats and launches were meeting and quarreling. The lordly sun still shone down, stifling hot, weighting limbs and shoulders as if with burning stones. She breathed out the scorching air, heavy and sour. How repellent were the sweaty workers wolfing down handfuls of rice, with their swollen chigger-infested toes, their scaly scabious knees, their trousers stiff with dirt and grease!

Suddenly Salimata shook with indignation. She had relaxed into a careless posture, her thighs had parted (because of this damned heat) and a miserable crouching wretch, with bare shoulders, a dribbling mouth and loose lips, was staring with great hare's eyes at the place between Salimata's legs. She immediately clamped her thighs together and rearranged her cloth. The man guiltily drew himself up on his long stork's legs, rose on creaking knees and hobbled away. Flies swarmed over his back and buttocks and his dusty unkempt hair. A starving madman? A sex-mad simpleton? Salimata's heart quailed. Chekura! Excision, rape, imprisonment! She should have given him a plateful of rice. Madmen, beggars and the unemployed don't have fifteen francs; they have poverty, suffering and bitterness, but also an open heart and God's love. Salimata should let the unemployed have rice on credit. Righteousness is more than wealth, and charity is one of God's laws.

'You who are out of work, call blessings down upon Salimata!'

'May God reward Salimata's good deeds twice over, and grant her many children!'

'May he hear you!'

Salimata laughed out loud with pleasure, like a bird displaying its shining throat in song. She counted her earnings again. Lots of coins! a lucky day! God and good fortune were with her. When you receive proof of God's goodness, you should offer a sacrifice. Sacrifice protects against misfortune, brings health, fruitfulness, happiness and peace. And the foremost sacrifice is to give; giving opens all hearts. And you never know, when you give, to whom you are giving. It might be a great sorcerer, one of God's elect, whose least word or gesture would be enough to make the most barren woman bear fruit.

'Come, all of you! here! eat!'

Salimata distributed platefuls of rice to the starving and the un-employed, until she had scraped the basin clean. Other starvelings and beggars came crowding round her, stretching out their hands, displaying their infirmities and sores. The basin was empty. Of course, there was still the money in the corner of her cloth; but she couldn't give that. It would be like giving away your eyes and hoping to use the back of your head. All the rich people, the big Europeans and Syrians, the presidents and secretary-generals should have fed the beggars and unemployed. But the rich don't know about this little market, and they never see or hear those in need. God sees and hears them, he knows them well, and keeps them going with the odd plateful of food during the day, and per-haps a fruit in the evening. But that's all, apart from what abounds in this city: the vast glitterirg expanse of the lagoon, with its salty foul-tasting water, and the sky blazing with sun or heavy with rain, for the poor who have nowhere to shelter and no fields to till. What can they do but roam about, filthy, muttering prayers and listening to the growls of their starving bellies?

Wretched beggars, ragged rogues, men long out of work, all rushed to stretch out their hands. Nothing! There wasn't a single grain of rice left. Salimata shouted that to them, and showed them as well. Couldn't they see that the dishes were empty? She held up the dishes one by one, so they could see inside, then stacked them again. Still they kept coming from all four corners of the mar-ket-place, and all crowded up close, murmuring prayers. They sur-rounded Salimata like a wall, shutting out the sun. As if from deep inside a well, she lifted her head and looked at them; they stopped muttering, and in stony silence held out their hands, displaying their infirmities. Their blank faces became cold and hard, their eyes went dark, their nostrils fluttered, their lips began to dribble. Others were still coming up to join them. They began to push and shove, stretching out their hands, and once more began to mutter prayers and the names of God. Then Salimata sensed the danger, understood what they meant to do. She panicked. Feeling that all was lost, she clutched her money tight and tried to rise and break out of the circle. The murmur grew louder, rose to a shout, and suddenly, as if at a signal, they all rushed at Salimata and attacked her, like a pack of mongooses; they robbed her, beat her, and before she had even had time to scream thrice they broke, scattered and disappeared in the market-place like a flock of birds into a thicket. They left Salimata lying alone in the sun and dust, her arms over her head, her cloth in disarray exposing her buttocks, her tightclamped thighs, her breasts. She quickly wrapped the cloth round her, covering her breasts, tidied herself. Her necklace and earrings had been torn off, and her dishes chipped. All her money, all her earnings gone! Hands had rummaged between her buttocks and thighs, under her breasts and belly.

After robbing Salimata they had scattered, but soon regrouped; with mocking hyena howls, they began to ransack the entire market. The women tried to stop them by covering their basins and sitting on the lids. But they rushed up, knocking over the women and their basins, and scooped up rice between their hands and forearms, even knelt and plunged nose, mouth and chin into the food lying on the ground, like animals.

The noise drew the attention of the police; whistles blew, the able-bodied thieves fled, the other brushed themselves off and wandered along like peaceful beggars or bystanders, with blank faces and deep-sunk eyes. But Salimata's ears hurt, and her bruised knees. She wept for her blouse torn under the left armpit, then rose, tidied herself, picked up the broken links of her necklace, looked for her head-tie, gathered and stacked her basins. She had recognized none of her assailants, but she had no doubt as to who they were; the men who had robbed and beaten her were the very men to whom she had given food. African beggars are like that; they are enemies of God. Salimata had often been warned. Too much open-handedness in the market-place causes evil deeds, riots and robbery; the paupers and rogues are too hungry, and there are too many of them.

All the generosity in the world would only leave them half-sated or envious. And a half-sated or envious beggar is a ferocious beggar, prepared to attack.

But Salimata had showed them the basins; they could see for themselves they were empty. She too was poor. Did God not see Salimata's poverty? Or is it that he never pities misfortune, because all misfortune is his doing? This was the most unlucky day Salimata had had in months. Best go and see the marabout, to find out the cause. Who knows, this bad luck might augur still worse to come. Her marabout (his name was Abdullahi) knew how to ward off the most dreadful blows of fate.

For the fourth time that day she crossed the lagoon, this time unhappy and indignant. Ah! the ingratitude of African beggars! Their wretched state was caused by God's just and righteous anger. Salimata would continue to give alms, but only to those truly in need, never again to such rogues, such lazy strays!

The boat broke through the many ripples of a lagoon sunk low beneath the sun's silent pressure. The little market and the European quarter, with its multi-storied white buildings, its green, blue, red windows, dwindled in the distance, and the African quarter loomed larger with its grey roofs and winding alleys. Beyond the African quarter, past where the lagoon ended near the bridge, the horizon was growing dark. Small fluffy clouds were floating up from the trees to lick the sky and the blazing sun, a sure sign of a storm. And here was the storm, it began to dance in the sky as Salimata, after landing at the wharf, took a short cut across the street of straw huts, turned left after the dispensary and came out in the Wolofs' courtyard. Gusts of wind tore through the alleys and rattled the roofs. Clouds swollen with triumph rushed like thieving beggars to assault the hapless sun. Salimata went through the door under the coconut palms; she had arrived safe in Abdullahi the marabout's compound. Let the sky split open now, and pour down all the water in its gourds and calabashes. Salimata didn't care. She had arrived where she wanted to be; she was at Abdullahi's, and the marabout was at home. Let the wind snatch up sand from the street now, and whistle through the tin roofs like a flock of weaver-birds.

'Did you have a peaceful morning?'

'Peace only! And you? has the day brought you peace?'

'Peace! God's will has been done. I wasn't expecting you, with this wind.'

42

There was a man there who had come to consult the marabout, crouched in a corner of the hut like a vulture asleep in a silk-cotton tree. He too greeted Salimata, invoked God's peace and blessings on her behalf. The marabout had almost finished with him. Salimata moved away and busied herself with a bit of tidying up, so as not to hear what the two men were whispering, the secrets of the marabout's power.

What would that man make of Salimata's relations with the marabout? She had come alone to see him, at a time when the storm would keep people indoors. Gossip? Gossip? But God knew there had never been anything more between her and the marabout than greetings exchanged and shared laughter. And they had known each other for months and months.

For a long time before she had met him, Salimata had heard from afar of the magical powers of the marabout Hadji Abdullahi. He had sorcery in the blood as other people have misfortune. Born in Timbuctoo, beyond the river at the desert's edge, among endless stretches of yellow sand and the harsh desert harmattan, where even the wind instils knowledge in men just as storms in our regions carry typhoid fever, Abdullahi could enter the invisible world as easily as his mother's room, and converse with spirits as if they were childhood friends. He need only point at a silk-cotton tree, for its trunk and branches to wither! For such a man, to make a child sprout even in the most arid belly, would be no trouble at all: a mere trifle! The only thing that had damped down her hopes and enthusiasms, was that Abdullahi's fees were high. He was a marabout for deputies, ministers, ambassadors and other powerful people for whom nothing is too dear, who could dress in robes made of banknotes, but whose feeling for humanity doesn't compel them to lend anything to the poor and the unemployed. The first time she visited the marabout, she explained that men who were out of work lived alone and were hungry, and she gave them food on credit; that she had no resources, nothing but great faith in God, compassion for the poor, and above all the affliction of sterility to be driven from her body.

'That's quite all right, Salimata!' the marabout had replied. 'Give what you can. Poverty is God's doing as well as wealth.'

Thereafter Salimata visited him again and again, they became better acquainted, and it reached a point where he could not do without her. The marabout lived alone. Sweeping, dusting, washing, tidying up, all that was a woman's job. Even if he did spend his nights in the heavens, and talk to spirits as if they were old friends, a man was still like a child. A swing of the hips, a flutter of the eyelids, a flashed smile and a peal of laughter were enough to soften and tame the imposing holy man. He bubbled with odd disconnected phrases, pronounced in a guileless tone of voice:

'He must cure her sterility; his own dignity was at stake. If the husband should prove irremediably incapable. Well then! Well then ... they would have to ... God judges our intentions too.'

Once desire had snagged the billy-goat's beard on the thorn-tree, the question of payment no longer arose. In fact, with Salimata Abdullahi even set aside his formal manner; a warm smile lit up his face, and he sometimes spoke like a small boy.

She prided herself on these attentions, and took advantage of them. Besides, Abdullahi was a fine figure of a man: strong and powerful as a Wasulu bull, with more life and verve to him than Fama, and possessed of knowledge as well as wealth. She came to consult him decked in ornaments, in smiles, in sparkling inquisitive glances. Responding, he had shaken out and emptied his most secret stores of knowledge, had called on the Invisible Ones time and time again to deliver Salimata's fertility; only a few more sacrifices, 'trifles', were needed now. While sweeping and tidying the room, she turned these thoughts over and over in her head. At last the marabout rid himself of his importunate client, who clung like a louse.

The fright that makes a puppy whimper when the scent of panther fills the night seized Salimata when the other man had left, and the marabout turned to her with eyes wide with anxiety and cheek-bones taut with fear.

'Salimata! Salimata! Salimata! Bitter days are ahead for you (may God temper them! may God avert them!). During last night's retreat, in the midst of my prayers and incantations, I saw things concerning you. First the weight of your sadness, then you yourself, and then blood, much blood, flowing over my arms and staining my robe. A raised knife, red with blood, was running like a hare. Shouts and cries of astonishment slowed its pace. And someone murmured: "He will strike and kill without a sacrifice".'

Deeply distressed, Salimata groaned with surprise and resignation. 'Wait! wait! you'll see'; and the marabout set about preparing divining spells. He performed three kinds: tracing signs in fine sand (to raise the dead), casting cowrie-shells (to invoke spirits); reading the Koran while gazing into a calabash full of water (to implore God).

First, the dead. With his index and middle finger together, he drew horizontal and vertical strokes. A silence. He rose, and rubbed his face with his cupped hands. Still silence. It must have been then that the shades of the dead entered the room and Abdullahi, for his cheeks swelled, his brows and lips tightened, his whole face grew rigid as if the man were about to die. Unconsciously, he made a few automatic gestures, as clumsy as an infant's first steps. He stared wildly at the signs traced in the sand. From his pursed lips burst oaths that rebounded from the walls, and among the oaths tumbled out the prestigious names of great ancestors. The names of great buried sorcerers! Salimata, exalted and transfixed, was riddled by oaths and invocations as if by bullets, and prayers and pleas rose within her like the wind:

'Shades of the ancestors! have mercy! save us!'

Her buttocks contracted and stiffened beneath the cloth that felt as light as a cobweb. For a moment it seemed as if the marabout had passed over to the dead; but only for a moment. He quickly came to life again, seized the pouch full of cowrie-shells, spilled out its contents, and once more grew rigid. Again he revived, but this time bristling with anger, with terrible words crowding to his lips; he gathered up the cowrie-shells, cast them again, and again stiffened. Silence! Silence! It was as if something were instilling silence into the being and substance of everything within the room. Outside there was the wind whining at the walls and roof, the rustle of clouds crowding the sky, the distant shouts of people running in the wind. The marabout came back to life, but this time little by little. First his fingers; he counted, then life reached his closed lips, which began to spout exclamations and oaths. Salimata admired him. Admiration flooded up her spine, as if after a hot and tumbled night, and drummed joyfully in her ears. Fear mingled in her with the desire for protection, as if she were a fledgling seeking to nestle under its mother's wing. Unconsciously she found herself leaning towards the marabout, as if obeying a call, and from her lips flew praise-singers' litanies:

'Benefactor! Man among men! O lion! Come forth, reveal yourself!'

Luckily for her self-respect, the marabout heard nothing; he could hear nothing, not even the sky sighing with pain at bringing forth fire.

Soon the returning tremor of life stung the soothsayer awake:

'That's it! that's the truth!' he exclaimed, and turning over the yellowed pages, he read a few lines, and called to Salimata:

'Look at your reflection in the calabash! Look! Look!'

This was shouted so violently that it was like a blow to her spine; she groaned deeply, and her cloth came undone. Obediently she bent over the calabash ...

'Tell me! what do you see in the water? Look closely! What do you see?'

'A cock, a big cock beating its wings and crowing,' murmured Salimata.

'Look again; look closely!'

'They're bringing a white sheep, it's a ram. Eh! Eh! it's gone now. Faces, grinning faces! Devil masks. Eh! Eh! black, red, mud from a creek, fine soft sand. Eh! it's all gone. Nothing more. Nothing. All gone.'

'Look again.'

'Nothing, nothing at all. Water, only water.'

'Nothing! really nothing! good, that's fine!' exclaimed the marabout, now relaxed, and added: 'Deceit says: tomorrow, inside the sack, or across the stream; but never, Here it is now; whereas truth shows the thing itself, with no need for further comment.'

'That's what there was. I saw the red cock and the white sheep,' replied Salimata.

'Your own mouth has said what sacrifices you must offer. I would add only that I advise you to make a sacrifice straight away. The newly traced signs, there in the sand, are calling for blood. That is my first piece of advice. The second concerns the sheep; but that sacrifice can be postponed, for a week or even a month.'

It had been a full, clear, straightforward demonstration of the marabout's techniques and powers. He was exultant, full of pride. She rubbed her eyes, troubled. Yet it wasn't a dream. There had been a red cock, beating its wings and stretching its neck to crow, and a white sheep, a ram with down-turned horns and a black muzzle.

'Let's do it right now. There's a poultry-vendor in the compound next door. The rain, yes, the rain will soon fall.'

Relaxed, persuasive, his voice like a small boy's, the marabout prolonged his words and gestures with smiles as broad as the Joliba river. In truth, one need only look, to know why! Salimata was born beautiful. Round, low-slung firm buttocks, even white teeth like a puppy's, she made one want to nibble at her; and that smooth, infinite expanse of skin, the marabout could not remember ever having touched, ever having penetrated its like!

She came back with a cock; the marabout seized it, stood it among the signs, stopped it from squawking and beating its wings. Resigned, the bird stretched its neck and clucked desperately.

They crouched facing each other, their hands holding the cock. The marabout stammered words of incantation. His voice was hoarse. Not for long, though; the awesome words cleared his throat, and burst forth like a volley of missiles, filling the room with mystery.

'Shades of the ancestors! Great spirits of the hills whose summits are always green! Spirits of the fathomless pools! God the all-forgiving, who covers and contains all! All of you! All!'

From his lips, opening and closing, sprang other awesome words, ringing and bright. The mysteries entered the cock, and reassured (O blasphemy!) it pecked at something in the sand.

'Something else to worry about!' thought Salimata. She was uncomfortable in that position, with cramps in her knees and in the small of her back; her cloth was slipping, she tightened it and tucked it in. What could be the misfortune that lay ahead for Salimata and her husband? They were poor, clothed in all the colours of poverty. Could it be a foolish accident, illness, death? At home in the village lived Salimata's old mother. May God preserve her for a long time yet! Fama's only close relative was a cousin he couldn't stand, not even for an overnight visit; his death would be a misfortune (what death is not!) but a lesser one. Something like an ant was crawling up Salimata's leg. She rested one hand on the ground and shifted her left foot, but worry and care still obsessed her.

The wind was still blowing, and shook the door and windows from time to time. The room was cluttered with miscellaneous objects: pots and calabashes, suitcases, a mat, near the bed some man's robes slung over a rope, and underneath the magic charms, red, yellow, green. The tin roof was low, and black with smoke. The room was stifling hot. Abdullahi was deep in a trance. The ritual words flowed easily between his teeth, his lips coined them and they burst forth, strong, vivid and awesome. They emerged and circled the room, then the forces summoned disappeared once more. Accepted! granted! You can always tell when a sacrifice is accepted. Everything flows smoothly. Once the first words of the incantation are uttered, the next words tumble out of their own accord. A misfortune definitely warded off! Praise be to God! Salimata deserved that favour, for her infinite compassion, faith and charity.

Yet a trifling incident almost spoiled everything. After crouching for such a long time, turning and stretching, it must be admitted that Salimata's posture had become highly provocative: her breasts rising into view, sinking, rising again; her thighs parted, dark, deep, alluring. Untimely lustful thoughts almost clouded the marabout's inspiration. Sacrilege! With a wave of his hand he dispelled such thoughts, sighed loudly, lifted his eyes to the roof beyond which lay God's heavenly abode, and resumed his incantation with a resounding *'Bissimilahi!'* God be praised, Salimata understood then; she pressed her thighs together, and resting one hand on the ground she tightened her cloth, tucked her breasts back into her blouse, and listened closely.

The way things were going, you couldn't tell what would happen next: the world was turned upside-down! Nowadays you had to perform sacrifices greater than you could possibly afford! Soon the little mouse would have to offer up a tomcat! A sheep! God must know that a sheep is a great deal to ask of Salimata and Fama: nearly two thousand francs. Even if day turned into night, out of all their hiding-places they'd never scratch up enough money to add up to ... Still more debts, then!

'Spirits of the dark quiet forests, of the hills that bring forth clouds, thunder and lightning! Shades of the renowned ancestors, backbone of life-giving earth, take, accept this sacrifice according to the will of God almighty, and deliver us from all misfortune, destroy all evil spells! Yes, all evil spells: those that rise from the south, those that come down from the north, those that spring from the east, those that blow from the west!'

The marabout had raised his voice to deliver that invocation; it broke as he was ending, and he whispered the rest:

'As a single tear-drop vanishes in a great river, may misfortune vanish with the wind that blows and dies away. Thanks be to God, the antelope leaps, its offspring will not crawl. May she who offers it acquire through this sacrifice the destiny of the little twig that survives a great forest fire.'

Together they lifted their cupped hands to their faces.

'Amen! Amen! Amen!'

'Hold its wings and feet, hold them tight ... Hold it down in the sand,' he ordered.

. He quickly unsheathed a knife with a curved point, burning bright, terrifying, like the knife the blacksmith's wife had used on her ... He slid it across the cock's throat, and pressed down; Salimata let out a low moan of horror.

'*Bissimilahi!*'

Blood spurted forth, the blood of excision, the blood of rape! The man put down the knife, seized the victim from the woman's grasp, and tossed it high and far out into the courtyard, into the wind. Like a baobab fruit the bird fell to the ground, and thinking it was free stretched towards the sky, once, twice, thrice, trying in vain to rise; its head and beak did not leave the ground. At last it gave a final squawk of agony, drummed the air with its wings, and disappeared in a whirlwind of dust, feathers and blood. Abdullahi and Salimata gazed intently at the sight.

She, struggling for breath, deaf and dizzy with the flash of superimposed colours: green and yellow in a mist of red, then all red; pain, and the swaying and singing at dawn; the field of excision at the foot of the mist-crowned hills, and the sun rising all red, drowned in blood, then the rape, night, the lamps bright and smoky and blown out, and the screams and the trampling and the bruises and weeping and shouts and robbery ...

The bird struggled once more, its movements growing weaker and weaker, until the final heave. It tried in vain to fly, and fell back, feet in the air and claws outspread.

'Sacrifice accepted! feet up! claws spread! clear signs of a sacrifice accepted, a wish granted!'

The marabout looked at Salimata, who relaxed and gleamed with smiles.

'God grant it be so!'

A last spasm shook the claw furthest to the left, the right thumb, the inner claw, each in turn. The quill-feathers spread too, one by one, and that was all. The wind became twice as strong, like the suffering and sun after excision, the night, tears and rape.

'Salimata, I swear it, that sacrifice has been accepted,' the marabout repeated.

Since noon, blown about by the wind and scorched by the sun, clouds had been growing, devouring the sky. Now flashes of lightning struck, shivering the sky into a thousand fragments from which thunder burst. The wind began to roar once more. Nothing could hold it back now: drops of rain as big as pigeon's eggs hammered the roofs and courtyard.

'Rain washing the ground after a sacrifice, that's very good. Another sign of a sacrifice accepted.'

'God give strength to your words! Thank you, Abdullahi, for turning away misfortune. But there is still sterility to haunt me; the talismans and medicines have not yet rooted it out. Take pity on me.'

Abdullahi did not answer. Once more the woman grew faint and chill with sadness and despair. Salimata and Abdullahi looked at each other. He with admiring glances, she with the curious contemplative eyes of a deer watching a hunter at the edge of the forest, poised for flight. Little by little she saw Abdullahi's gaze change, the skin tighten over his cheek-bones, the veins in his forehead swell. Still they looked at each other.

The door was closed tight. Outside the wind howled and the rain beat down. In such a storm, no one, no one at all could turn up unexpectedly. So they were alone, quite alone. He had warded off the misfortune that threatened her (a good deed by a manly man!). She had tidied his room with care (like a dutiful wife). Together they had sacrificed the cock. The red cock lay cooling in a basin. Blood had spurted, but for each of them the blood had a different colour, a different scent. For him, the colour of tenderness, the scent of desire for smooth skin, rounded buttocks and white teeth. For her, the colour of daybreak and excision, the scent of tension and terror.

'Lend your ears, Salimata, and heed what I say! Words untangle themselves like the feathers of that cock (he pointed at the basin). God has ordained marriage, it is a totem. But for a woman, a child is more than anything else; the aim of life is to bring forth offspring. Truth, like a ripe red pepper, reddens the eyes but does not blind them. Some destinies are ordained by God once and for all time. Your husband, I say this with a clear tongue and conscience, will never make a woman fruitful. He is as sterile as a rock, as dust, as the harmattan wind. That alone is the truth. Anything else is a lie, and there is no more good in lies than there is blood in a cricket,' he concluded.

Outside raged the wind and the rain. Inside the room, everything seemed to cry out over and over:

'The husband! The husband cannot make you fruitful!'

The tongues, the eyes, the ears of other people, of the city, of the world were far away. Four eyes! four ears! and no more. And, 'the husband! the husband cannot make you fruitful!'

'Come!' murmured the marabout.

She backed away. Like a python, he twisted, swayed, attempted a smile. She looked at him; from far within her rose the mists of excision and rape, and everything changed; the marabout's eyes rolled and flashed with Chekura's savage nature; his nostrils flattened and became hideous, like Chekura's.

'Why? Why hesitate? give me your hand!' he added.

She stood there, tense and breathless.

Outside the wind and rain were still at it. Nothing could take them by surprise. But memories rose to assault her. Proud and smiling she had gone forth to the field of excision. Torn by pain, she had met misfortune and shed blood like the cock; there was pain, the scent of sacrifice and worship, and then Abdullahi the marabout, facing her. She stared at him: no doubt about it. Round his neck rose Chekura's iron collars, and his robe had turned the colour of Chekura's clothes.

'Come! Come!'

He knew and thought of only one thing: he and the woman were alone together. He could see only a round glowing female, hesitant but submissive, and could feel only the desire that moved and heated him. He pulled hard at her cloth.

'Leave me alone or I'll scream!'

He smiled. No! She wouldn't scream; he held fast and pulled harder; the woman fell back sprawling on the bed; all he needed to do was leap on her. But he could not, for she screamed with rage and fury and leapt up in a frenzy, as if possessed; snatched up a stool, an amulet, a calabash to pelt the frightened marabout, who ran about shouting 'It was God's doing! It was God's doing!' The knife with the curved tip was lying on the ground; armed with it, she pursued him and cornered him between the bed and the suitcases. In Salimata's eyes blazed rape, blood and Chekura, and her heart heaved with vengeful anger. The curved blade struck his left shoulder. The man in turn howled like a wild beast, growled like thunder. She took fright and fled through the doorway, waded three or four steps in the rain, snatched up the basins and the sacrificed chicken and ran out.

Behind her, the marabout was still heating the room with his howls. She plunged into the rain, ran across the compound and out into the street. A cool wind was blowing; a light rain was falling, in widely spaced drops the size of shea-nuts. The drops rattled on the basin and on her shoulders. There was mud everywhere, lying thick about the houses, flowing in ditches and on to the road. No one in the street! That was lucky. No one would see the fear hidden in her heart, or the shame plain on her face. To her left lay a narrow alley. She entered it, to weep over her misfortune and to hide her face, the face of a woman who would never have a child because the only man she could bear to sleep with was sterile. She had the sacrificed cock with her. Further on she came to a small hill; at the top there was a crossroads, a narrow bridge, and a ravine through which foaming water roared. She stopped near the railing of the bridge, took out the dead chicken and flung it into the torrent, where it spun about and was carried away. She walked in the same direction, breathing heavily. The rain had stopped here, there was only a light drizzle. The sky was shimmering. For a long time she trudged after the sacrificed chicken. She was thinking that all the children she had dreamt and longed for were now flowing beyond her grasp, drifting away with the bloodied cock, gone forever. She was fated to be barren until she died.

PART TWO

5 He was tethered by the genitals, and death was closing in; luckily the moon came to the rescue

The ultimate affront, that neither hurries, grows weary nor forgets, is called death. It had carried away cousin Lasina from the village. Yes, the cousin; and although he was the man who by intrigue, magic spells and sacrificial offerings had usurped Fama's place as chief of Horodugu, his death was a misfortune. Recriminations must be silenced. A dead man is for God alone to judge, and the duty of his surviving relatives is to organize a respectable funeral. Fama decided to go to the village for the funeral ceremonies; he visited all the Malinke households in the city, to break the news of his cousin's death and announce his own departure. May God never cease to pour blessings and strength on the Malinke community in the capital city! Each Malinke outdid the other in generosity. Everyone took out money to give. Altogether there was more than enough for the journey, and for an imposing funeral. Fama could leave.

Early one morning he turned up at the road transport station, accompanied by Salimata and many other Malinke. The lorries travelling north were lined up in noisy ranks. Fama got into the lorry driven by Wedrago.

'No! No!' they shouted. 'Get out, grandad! Get into the one that's first in line!'

The man who was doing the shouting introduced himself:

'Delegate of the national union of road carriers.' Fama had best get out, without arguing. 'That's the way it is.' Road carriers' union or bastards' union, Fama couldn't care less. He stood up, pulled out his knife, and in spite of Salimata's screams threatened the delegate and insulted everyone, the delegate and all the bastards in the union, their father and the mother of Independence. The delegate backed away and left 'that crazy Malinke' alone.

They started off, and as they left the city Fama congratulated himself for having bared the panther's fangs of a true Dumbuya. He had been right, twenty times over, to have recourse to insults and threats in order to stay in Wedrago's lorry. You need only watch the others overtake, and see the drivers, head and one arm thrust out the cab window, shouting 'To hell with death!' as they met and passed other vehicles in a din of hooting horns and jangling metal. Another lorry would start up a concert of horns behind you, draw level with you and swing over towards the ditch, flinging to one side the passengers sitting huddled on their luggage; then overtake, swerve back in right in front of you, speed uphill and disappear downhill. The roadside bristled with the skeletal remains of countless lorries, like carcasses whose innards had been devoured by vultures. Wedrago, on the contrary, was as cautious as a chameleon; when avoiding a fault in the road or entering a curve, he would murmur a thousand prayers mingling God's names and the ancestors'. Fama too prayed that the journey might go well.

They were crossing the stretch of savanna that surrounded the lagoons. Shrubs clung to the slopes of endless rolling hills. It was morning. The sun had just appeared, and was hurriedly dissolving clouds and sweeping them away, before rising higher to reign over a true harmattan day. Fama was worried and melancholy. He was leaving behind Salimata, the capital, all his friends, all the ceremonies and palavers, and he did not know when he would be able to return. He was head of the tribe now that his cousin was dead. Should he accept the position and stay in the village, or decline and return to the city? Fama had not yet decided. Of course, he would consult soothsayers, offer sacrifices and choose the most auspicious course. Whatever he decided, Fama would have many difficulties to deal with; he wanted to think, so as to be ready to unravel them when they appeared. Unfortunately, though, he was not alone. There were many other travellers in Wedrago's lorry, and Fama's three neighbours were far too talkative.

Fama had to tell them where he was going. His neighbour exclaimed in surprise. His name was Jakite, and he was from Horodugu; of course he knew Fama's village and the Dumbuya family, had known Fama's cousin, had heard of Fama. 'Peace be with you, Fama!' he said before continuing. How many seasons was it since

Fama had last been home? Years? Not for years? In that case, there were many unpleasant surprises waiting for him there. He, Jakite, had fled his village; his village was in the part of Horodugu that lay in the People's Republic of Nikinai, and Nikinai was socialist. Did Fama know how he, Jakite, had escaped? No? It was thanks to the moon! yes, the moon that moves through the sky.

His father had been a wealthy and respected man (sixty head of cattle, three lorries, ten wives and only one son, he himself, Jakite). Then came Independence, socialism and the one-party system. Jakite's father, who belonged to the opposition, was summoned and informed that his party was now defunct; he would have to join the one existing party, the NDL. He joined, and paid dues for himself, his family, his cattle and his three lorries. The next day they called him in again; he would have to pay party dues for every year elapsed since the NDL was created: ten years' dues for himself, his son, his ten wives, his sixty cattle and his three lorries. He paid up.

A few months later, hot on the heels of the single-party system, came self-help. Jakite's father was to hand over his lorries for use in building a bridge for the village. He placed his lorries at the party's disposal, but since there was no petrol, the NDL youth set fire to them. The indignant old man resigned himself to his loss, and even affected an ironic smile (in any case, since Independence there were no roads and no petrol).

The party officials turned up again another day: the bridge was being built by self-help, and neither Jakite nor his father were taking part. The old man reminded them that it was harvest-time, that his son could not leave his fields and cattle. They left, but that evening when Jakite, returning home with his herd, crossed the bridge, the NDL youth were lying in wait for him; they leapt out and attacked him, pinioned him, pulled off his trousers, attached a rope to his genitals and tied him to one of the posts of the bridge, like a dog. Jakite's father ran to implore the party secretary-general, who replied that since socialism was to bring to an end the exploitation of man by man, nobody should set foot on a bridge he had not helped build. The old man begged for mercy, but he could not be moved: socialism was socialism!

Jakite's father went home, then returned and ordered him to go and release the victim; the secretary-general burst out laughing. Then the old man went mad, raised his shot-gun and fired full in his chest; the secretary-general collapsed. Other villagers came running, Jakite's father fired again, and panic spread. It was night-time. The demented old man went from compound to compound, and gunned down one after the other the assistant secretary-general, the treasurer and two other party members. The whole village took refuge in the bush. He went to the creek, unbound his son, untied the rope round his genitals and set him free. Luckily, there was a moon that night. For three moonlit nights Jakite was able to find his way through the bush, avoiding snakes and wild beasts, until he reached the border. His father had been tried and shot.

There was a moment's silence. They had left behind the lagoon savanna, and were now crossing a densely forested zone. As one bend followed another, the exhausted passengers were flung from side to side, and Fama felt dizzy and nauseated. He cleared his throat, spat out sticky spittle with a sickly taste of baobab sap, then sat up.

His left-hand neighbour took up the palaver. He too had fled socialism; his name was Konate, and he was a Bambara. Yet all his features were those of a Fula: tribal tattoo-marks, the dry brittle look of a tree in the dry season, and ears like an aardvark. He repeated himself constantly. He had escaped in time, just in time, since three days later they had changed banknotes and all the traders had been irremediably ruined.

Konate missed his country, he loved it and felt that socialism would be a good thing later on; but as with all big babies, the birth and first steps were hard, too hard: famine, shortages, forced labour, prison ... It was in order to temper the harshness of social-ism that he hung about the borders, dealing illegally in black-mar-ket currency and smuggled goods. It was really for God, love of humanity and patriotism that he was travelling, in spite of all the risks lying in wait at the gates of socialism.

Sery, who was sitting opposite Fama, spoke next. He, Sery, knew the secret of peace and happiness in Africa. Sery was Wedrago's apprentice, and since the start of the journey, clinging to the back of the lorry, he had not stopped wriggling about, singing and com-plaining. His boss drove too slowly, a real chameleon. If he were at the wheel, the lorry would have covered many more miles by now. He glowed with youth and health. He had plump hips and arms and a neck like a young bull, bulging from a shirt and trousers torn and stiff with grease; and the magnetic face of a young wild animal, with a puppy's round eyes and white teeth.

'Do you know what causes wars and misery in Africa? No? Well, it's quite simple; it's because Africans don't stay at home,' Sery explained.

He himself had never left the Ebony Coast to settle in another country and deprive its inhabitants of work, whereas other people had come to his country. The French colonizers brought along people from Dahomey and Senegal, who knew how to read and write and were French citizens or else Catholics; smarter, more civilized, harder-working Africans than the native inhabitants of the country, who belonged to Sery's tribe.

'The white colonizers gave them all the jobs and all the money, and with that money the Dahomeyans bedded our girls, married the prettiest ones, took over our best land, lived in the tallest houses; they cut our children's throats as offerings to their fetishes, and French justice didn't interfere because they themselves were the judges and lawyers. Whenever there was a new post created, they brought someone from Dahomey to fill it, and whenever someone was sacked or out of work, it was always one of our own people. This was how it was,' Sery demonstrated with his hands, 'the Europeans on top, then the Dahomeyans and Senegalese, and we were just nothing, lying underfoot'.

So, as soon as Independence came, the Sery rose up and attacked the Dahomeyans.

'First we took back our women, then we beat their children and raped their sisters before their very eyes, before plundering their goods and setting their houses on fire. Then we chased them down to the shore. We wanted to drown them, to see the waves wash them ashore with swollen bellies, unrecognizable, like dynamited fish. Luckily for them the French troops intervened, herded them into the harbour and guarded the entrance with tanks. So the Dahomeyans boarded ship and left. Once they had left and independence had come, the country was really in fine shape. There were jobs and houses for everyone. So our students and intellectuals said we should get rid of the French; that would bring us a lot more in the way of houses, goods and money. But that was difficult, because of the French troops; besides, it wouldn't have been a good thing, because without the French there would be no jobs and we were tired of being out of work.'

That was why the Sery had refused. But now things were going wrong again, because other Africans wouldn't stay at home; they kept coming to the Ebony Coast, Nago from the south, Bambara and Malinke fleeing socialism, Mossi from the north, Hausa from the east.

The Mossi and Hausa could be tolerated, they came to work, and took the jobs the native inhabitants didn't want, the unpleasant or dangerous ones. But when the others arrived, especially the Nago, they were as wretched and threadbare as an orphan's only pair of drawers, and even dirtier. And they never turned up alone, always with their wives who bred like lizards, and their brats more numerous than two litters of mice; they also brought along their beggars, their blind men, their cripples, their madmen, their liars and thieves to invade our public squares and surround our mosques, our churches, our markets. Furthermore, whether handicapped or not, the Nago never worked, but hung about factories, workshops and shops with outstretched hands.

'Out of charity we gave them alms; since they were as dried-up as dead snakes and didn't need food, they saved up what we gave them to buy cigarettes, and turned up again to sell them to us on tick; soon it was rice, shirts, shoes they sold on tick, and they ended up advancing us half our salaries and charging money-lenders' rates of interest. They were rich; they came to live in our houses, and in less than a week our compounds were as disgusting as their brats' unwashed faces, as stinking as their brats' unwiped arses. So we left them to it. They bought the compounds, fixed them up, left, rented them out and started on other compounds. That's how they managed to take over the whole city. Our leaders began to use them as fronts for buying, selling, borrowing. It's the Nago who can get loans from the French and the Syrians; we're the ones who work, and it's foreigners who earn the money. We don't like that at all. Will we have to start killing again, driving people into the sea? It's not nice,' concluded Sery.

That was why he said that Africa would know peace when every African stayed at home.

The passengers were all silent. The lorry was on a straight stretch of road, dazzling hot in the sun; they had crossed the Budomo river, and the trees were smaller.

'So my words have been greeted with silence, like the old grandmother's fart among respectful grandchildren,' remarked Sery, with a burst of laughter that drew no response.

He looked up, and was startled to see everyone staring at him in weary amazement. People's lips were drawn and pressed tight, and their ears heard only the motor's roar.

60

Now Fama began to think. When he had shown Salimata the letter announcing the death, she had exclaimed:

'God, have mercy on the deceased! Grant him a better resting-place!'

Then she rose from her stool and started banging her pots and pans about, as if ... What was she after? She came back, her hands empty, her eyes full of tears:

'Well? what do you plan to do, Fama?'

'Nothing. I'll just go up there for the funeral, then come back.'

'Do you really intend to come back to the city? To take up this life again? Fama, tell me the truth,' she begged.

Fama did not know the truth. He was now the incumbent leader of the Dumbuya tribe. What honour, what power that had meant before the European conquest! All the Dumbuya mothers had poured out libations and offered sacrifices, that their womb might bring forth the child that would be chief of the dynasty. In a world turned upside-down, Fama had inherited an honour without the means to uphold it, like a headless snake. To be chief of a starving tribe means only famine and a gourdful of worries. Fama, you should prepare to refuse, to tell them no.

The lorry was panting up a hill. Behind them disappeared a curve as like the curve they were approaching, that shimmered in the heat, as two paw-prints of the same beast. A wooded hill emerged from ashen clouds drifting in a sunken sky. You lost your bearings in this unchanging landscape. And after sitting for so long on benches as hard as stone, your buttocks were sore, your calves and thighs heavy as if weighted with mortars, and pins and needles climbed up to your knees.

You'll never escape them! they won't let you turn down your inheritance. The village people's tongues are persuasive, honey-sweet. But what could he do? Should he give up the journey and return to the city? No, that's impossible, quite unthinkable! In that case, be prepared to inherit the position. It's like a person's hand: there are only two sides, palm and back. Either you give up the trip, or you go there to inherit everything, even the women.

The women too! The dead man had left four widows, the four most substantial items of his estate, two of them old women the deceased himself had inherited. Those two will surely not marry again. After burying two husbands, you must feel that men have nothing more to offer you, no more juice or flavour. But the two others! Especially Mariam. As a girl, Mariam had been offered to

Fama, because everyone deplored his wasting away in arid sterility with Salimata. But nothing came of it. In the first place, because of Salimata's sarcastic remarks.

'Fama, Fama,' she would say, 'just think, take a look at yourself. Do you really think you can mount the two of us? With me, it's as much of a job as drawing water from the top of a hill. And those aches and pains in your back and sides, after every night ...'

Besides, that was the time when trade was declining, and politics took up all of his time. In other words, Fama had turned down Mariam because he'd neither the loins nor the money. In the village, people had spoken ill of Fama: a legitimate son of a chief, huddled under the wing of a sterile woman – a degenerate! And they had given Mariam to Cousin Lasina. They had had one or two children.

6 Pacing away in the night of the heart and the shadow of the eyes

After a curve, the surfaced road came to an end. From here on it was just a dirt road, with dust screening off the rear view, dust clustering in all the trees and grasses of the bush, and on the roofs of huts; the road flung it up, the exhaust spewed it out, and dust hovered inside the lorry, filling eyes, throat and nose. As the lorry bumped along the uneven road, the passengers were constantly being flung against each other, their heads hitting the roof. You had to tighten your jaws; if you talked, with all this rattling about you might bite off your tongue. A trip like this was back-breaking for a man of Fama's age. But what could he do? Both God and custom enjoined attendance at a cousin's funeral ceremonies.

The road wound slowly upwards. After living together for nearly twenty years, Fama and Salimata knew each other as well as the crocodile and the little carp that lived in the same pond. If Fama were to marry Mariam after the funeral and return with her to the city, he could readily imagine how Salimata would react. A hypocrite, to begin with she would deck herself with smiles and sweetness, overflow with false solicitude and kind attentions. 'A woman beyond reproach', you might think. Oh no! Not at all! Just wait! One evening, for no reason at all, she would return home silent, as if crushed by the weight of countless worries. And it would begin. Huddled in a corner, she would drone out songs about human suffering, the suffering of wives who feed, clothe and house their husbands, the suffering of wives with ungrateful husbands, the duties of husbands, sterility, the obligation to provide each wife with her own room, and so on and so forth ... in other words, a series of bad-tempered outbursts that in the end would annoy and provoke Fama.

'What did you say, Salimata?'

'I wasn't speaking to anyone in particular,' she would reply.

And it would go on like that. An intolerable atmosphere. Quarrels, anger, the whole household topsy-turvy. Today insults, tomorrow blows: an impossible situation, like sitting on a swarm of red ants. It would end in a break-up. Fama, best consider, think carefully before marrying Mariam. Unless! unless! unless! you decide to stay in the village...

'A fire! a fire!'

The cry startled Fama. Yes, that's what it was: a huge bushfire, like a storm. Whirling flames crackled, rumbled and hissed, and everything that could, fled before them. The road was swarming with grasshoppers.

They soon passed through the fire and left behind the sinister clouds of smoke. The sight had roused and refreshed Fama, but the landscape continued dull, without variety.

As a little boy, Fama used to go digging for rats with his playmates: when the first one rushed out, they would shout, 'A rat!' but when more followed, they would just call out, 'Another one!' Fama blinked; another one came by. Another village just like the first village they had passed through: the creek, the round huts with the same thatched roofs, the sacred wood, the lazy ruminating cattle and the bare-arsed children with swollen gourd-bellies, always frightened, always squalling. After the village, he blinked again: another stretch of bush crushed by the sun, the same harmattan horizon, the same clear sky; then another bend to the right, another leaning shea-tree with its pack of chattering monkeys in full flight, always startled, always mocking. Then another straight stretch of road, pausing at the top of a hill before the descent into another village. Fama dozed; they were driving along without getting anywhere, and he was tired, as weary and worn out as the seat of a street urchin's pants. Finally, at the crest of a laterite hill, he blinked, and was startled to see Binja appear in a halo of dust: their resting-place for the night, an end to aches and pains. God be praised!

Smoke rose from the huts that stood among mango- and flame-trees, at the foot of two hills as neatly rounded as Salimata's breasts as a girl. The hills touched a faint blue, copper-tinged sky; between them, on the horizon, the already muted sun was dying in a daub of flame-trees. Evening had come. Small houses ringed with red hid among the leafless mango-trees, blending with them in the distance.

The honey-coloured streets, crackling with dry leaves, wound through tufts of sisal. They drove through the administrative quarter. The passengers disembarked in the Malinke quarter, where the huts were crowded together in a smell of smoke and cow-dung.

Just at that moment the sun sank behind a hill, and from the other hill came mist and darkness.

Night enfolded the town.

All Binja greeted Fama as an honoured guest, and treated him as if he were president for life of the republic, the party and the government; in other words, he was given the welcome due a Malinke married to Salimata, who was from Binja. Caller succeeded caller in front of his hut, then dishes of *toh* and rice were lined up in his honour, even a chicken and a kid tied to a stake. After last prayer, the palaver began. Fama, reclining full-fed on his mat, was prepared to unsheath his tongue and lash out with a cut-and-thrust denunciation of the bastard politicians and suns of Independence. But they cut him short. The republic's single party forbade villagers to listen to anything people arriving from the capital city might say about politics. God be praised, there are as many ways of talking as there are bastards! So Fama dredged up his memories, and asked about all those who had lately died, married, given birth and been cuckolded. And the palaver flowed freely, while moths flew out of the night to dash themselves to death against the paraffin lamp in their midst, and mosquitoes whined and droned in and out of the shadows. It was (Fama noted with pleasure) a true, unbastardized African night, crackling with all the sounds of the harmattan season: crickets chirping, hyenas howling, and of course dogs responding with an unending din of barking and yapping. Beyond the circle of light only one star sparkled in the sky. You had to lean over to glimpse others between the roofs. All the huts across the way had their shutters down. After all that sun and the incredibly long journey, Fama's back began to stiffen like a rod of iron, and he yawned as if his mouth would crack open at the corners. The visitors understood that sleep had overcome him.

'Spend the night in peace! May God guard your journey's course from foolish accidents and bad luck!'

The circle broke up.

*　　*　　*

Fama was awakened in the middle of the night by a tingling sensation in his buttocks, back and shoulders, that smarted as if he had lain in a ditch full of couch-grass. The bamboo bed was bristling with mandibles, alive with bedbugs and fleas. Would it be long until morning? Fama listened to the night.

The hyenas had stopped howling, but you could tell from the frightened whimpering of dogs with their tails between their legs, scratching at closed shutters, that they were still there, lying in wait behind the houses; the whole village must stink of them. From time to time you heard the rustle of night-birds taking flight from a tree. Then there were other cries as well, beasts whose names Fama had forgotten and digested during his twenty stupid years in the city. The lamp's flame trembled. It was good that it should be there, for in these bush villages it is always dangerous to sleep, that is to say, for a Malinke, to set free your soul, without a little light left burning to ward off other wandering souls, bad spells and evil spirits. Hell and damnation! Fama was annoyed at not being able to sleep, and told himself that he ought to be using this time to think about his future. Consider serious things, you legitimate descendant of the Dumbuya. The last of the Dumbuya! Are you, yes or no, the last; the last descendant of Suleyman Dumbuya? These suns overhead, these politicians, all these shameless people, these liars and thieves, are they not the bastard desert where the great Dumbuya river must disappear? And Fama began to reflect on the history of the dynasty, in order to interpret things and through exegesis of tradition to discover his own destiny.

One Friday at the hour of third prayer, Suleyman, called Moriba out of deference, arrived at Tukoro with a column of Koranic students. The chief of Tukoro recognized and greeted him. They were awaiting him; his coming had been announced.

'A marabout, a great marabout will come from the north at the hour of *urebi*. Keep him! Don't let him go! Offer him land and a house. The power of the whole province will go wherever he and his descendants dwell.'

The chief of Tukoro had recognized him by his height, like that of the silk-cotton tree, by the colour of his skin (he was to be taller and fairer than any man in the village) and by his horse (he was to arrive on a spotless white steed). He wanted to detain him, so that he would settle in Tukoro, but in those days the harvest festival lasted eight days, and during those eight days masks and fetishes danced and shouted through the village streets and squares, and women and strangers were forbidden to step outside. The chief of Tukoro summoned his guest:

'Great marabout! The drums will soon sound for the harvest festival. Have your women and disciples prepare a week's supply of food and water for you and yours.'

'Honourable chief! Allow us to withdraw and spend the festival period in our fields ...,' replied Suleyman.

'Very well, marabout, but come back after the festival,' said the chief.

But they never returned. The fields lay between two villages, and the neighbouring chief objected.

'If it has been ordained that power will prosper where Suleyman resides, let him settle between our two territories.'

Suleyman and his students built a large encampment called Togobala (great camp) and founded the Dumbuya tribe, of which Fama was the sole remaining legitimate descendant. The story of Suleyman is the story of the Dumbuya dynasty.

There is another version.

Suleyman and his escort arrived in Tukoro, one Friday at the hour or *urebi*. The chief of Tukoro, drunk on millet beer, lay asleep among his subjects, who shook him, saying:

'The great marabout on the white steed, with a numerous retinue, is crossing the village.'

He just muttered, 'Let me sleep!'

Once the chief had sobered up, a messenger was immediately despatched. But Suleyman could no longer turn back, he was halfway between two territories; he set up camp on the spot where the messenger had caught up with him, and there built many straw huts (*togobala*).

Whatever the true story may be, Togobala spread and prospered like an anthill, a source of wisdom where all who were parched with the thirst for knowledge and religion would come to drink. Suleyman's lineage flowed freely on, strong, honoured and admired, rich in great scholars and holy men, until the conquest of Horodugu by the Muslim Malinke from the north. As they despised the Bambara who were its original inhabitants, the conquerors offered to make the descendant of Suleyman Dumbuya the country's ruler. His name was Bakary. And Bakary ought not to have accepted. The Bambara had showered honours and land upon his ancestors, and power over a province is to be won by arms, blood and fire; power acquired by ingratitude and cunning is unlawful, and it does not last, but dies out amidst great misfortunes. All unlawful power, like thunder, bears within it the bolt of lightning that will consume it in the end.

Bakary sought guidance, prayed, worshipped God and the ancestors. One night a voice called out:

'Thank you, Bakary! Thank you for your offerings! Take power! That which is written will be enacted with without fail, but because of your piety, special terms can be arranged. Your lineage will flow, dwindle, then dry up and disappear, like a powerful stream that pours down from the mountainside, waxes great, then wanes to a trickle and dies out in a sandy desert valley, far from rivers and the sea.'

'I renounce power,' replied Bakary, chilled.

'Take it. Your lineage will not come to an end tomorrow, nor the day after, nor any day soon. It will end when the sun never sets, when bastards and sons of slaves bind all the provinces together with threads, ribbons and wind, and rule over them; when everything is cowardly and shameless, when families are...'

'Yes! Yes! Thank you, I understand,' exclaimed Bakary as if inspired: my lineage will end on the Day of Judgement.

And Bakary took power over all the wealthy provinces, all the lands of Horodugu. The Dumbuya became the honoured chiefs of Horodugu, that had now been split between two different republics. A pity! A pity that ancestor Bakary did not wait and listen to the end. The voice would have continued to describe the day when the Dumbuya dynasty would end. Fama was afraid. He was the only true descendant left, a sterile man living on alms in a city where the sun never sets (electric lights shone in the capital city all night long), where bastards and sons of slaves rule in triumph, having bound the provinces together with wires (the telephone!), ribbons (roads!), and wind (speeches and the wireless!). Fama was afraid of the night, of the journey, of the funeral, of Togobala, of Salimata, of Mariam and of himself. Afraid of his fear.

Morning came and went too soon. It was the second day of the journey. Everything seemed to happen more quickly. Like a chief of old, the harmattan mist took over the hills, roads and bush. But there wasn't time to complain. The sun set itself free, and had soon evaporated, melted, cleared and dispelled it all. The lorry moved quickly, and the stones cast up in its wake, amid the attendant cloud of dust, made the dead leaves rattle at the roadside. Villages passed and disappeared in the dust. Their names drummed a beat of sorrow in Fama's breast. The lorry was already on the land of the province of Horodugu. Everything both seen and unseen, heard and unheard, scented and beyond reach of scent, everything: the land, the trees, the waters, the men and beasts, everything around them should have belonged to Fama, like his own wife. What a terrible, changing, baffling world this was! Within him rose voices praising the power of his dynasty, the courage of his valiant ancestors. As the lorry rounded a bend, he could hear them mount a thunderous charge against the bastard unlawful rule of presidents of the republic and single parties. The ancestors would have had the heart and strength for that, they were true men and absolute rulers. The dynasty that ruled over all the land, all the inanimate objects and living beings of Horodugu, had bred virile and intelligent warriors. There was not one grain of sand (the lorry was crossing a plain scorched by recent bush-fires), not one hand's-breadth of this plain that their horses' hooves had left untrodden. Throughout this land they had attacked, killed and conquered.

They came to the last village of the Ebony Coast; beyond it, before entering the Socialist Republic of Nikinai, was a customs post. There Fama gave way to a fit of rage, the kind that makes a serpent tremble like a leaf, its throat choked with insults left unspat. A bastard, a real one, a shameless forest brat whose mother surely never knew a scrap of loincloth nor the married state, dared to stand there on his own two testicles and say that Fama, a foreigner, could not pass without an identity card! Did you hear that? Fama a foreigner on the soil of Horodugu! Fama ordered him to repeat what he had said. The fat, round, pot-bellied little customs man, all rigged out from chest to toes in gun-belt and puttees, calmly repeated his words, and even added a few remarks about revolution, independence, the removal of chiefs from office, and freedom. Fama exploded, cursed and shouted so loudly that the whole post shook. Fortunately, the man in charge was a Malinke, therefore a Muslim and able to distinguish gold from copper. Fama was appeased with all due honours and apologies.

'He's a descendant of the Dumbuya.'

'I don't give a f... about Dumbuya or Konate,' the son of a savage replied.

Fama, sweating and out of breath, pretended not to hear, and got back into the lorry.

Fama's anger suddenly left him, like a swift harmattan whirlwind.

69

They were crossing stretches of bush Fama had ridden through time and time again in his youth, and his heart was warmed by the thought of those childhood mornings. From everywhere appeared forgotten sounds, smells, and shadows; even a familiar sunlight filled the air. His youth! His youth! He came upon it everywhere, saw it galloping on the white charger far away on the horizon, heard it come and go through the trees, smelled it, tasted it. He rejoiced in his ancestors' deeds, until suddenly his heart began to beat more quickly and he grew sad, his joy cut short by the return of last night's fears, sorrow for the Dumbuya lineage and his own destiny. From deep within him rose melancholy tunes, and he repeated over and over to himself this Malinke wedding-song:

> You cannot know the worth of a father, a father
> Until you find the house without a father,
> You cannot see a mother, a mother
> More excellent than gold
> Until you find the mother's hut empty of the mother,
> Then you pace, pace away
> In the heart's night and the eyes' shadow
> And turn away to shed a flood of burning tears.

Thereupon appeared, outlined against a radiant harmattan sky, the crown of the silk-cotton tree of Togobala! Togobala, his native village! The same vultures (the bastards, who called Fama a vulture!), surely the very same vultures as when he was young took flight from the silk-cotton tree to patrol the village indolently from above. Cattle, goats, women bearing water-jars on their head; then came the houses.

For the sake of his ancestors' renown, Fama rubbed his eyes to make sure he wasn't mistaken. Of the Togobala of his childhood, the Togobala he bore in his heart, there was nothing left, not even the whiff of a fart. All the same, in twenty years the world hadn't turned upside-down. But this was what remained. Here and there one or two tumbledown sun-baked huts, isolated like anthills on a plain. Among the ruins of former compounds lay rubbish heaps and stretches of grass grazed by beasts, burnt by fire and dried by the harmattan.

Children swarmed out of the huts and rushed towards the lorry, crying 'Mobili!', tottering on millet-stalk legs above which swayed their dusty little gourd-bellies. Fama was reminded of little lizards. At last a landmark! Fama recognized the baobab in the market-place. It too had suffered and was decrepit; from its scarred ashen trunk, bare leprous branches reached towards the arid sky, a sky haunted by the dry-season sun and by the flights of wheeling vultures, on the look-out for carrion and the leavings of people who relieved themselves behind the houses. The lorry stopped.

'Welcome! Welcome, Fama!'

Villagers of all ages were rushing up, all as gaunt and parched as catfish in their second season, their skin rough and dusty as a lizard's, their eyes red and rheumy with conjunctivitis.

With the supple stride of his panther totem, with royal gestures and majestic nods (a pity his robe was so dusty and wrinkled!), escorted by a retinue of villagers and swarming children, Fama reached the dwelling-place of the Dumbuya ancestors. Just then, a piercing cry rang out: the signal for weeping and wailing in honour of the dead man. Howling as if possessed, all the women flung themselves on the ground and rolled about in the dust. The noise drew other women to join in the keening, and spread throughout the village. The dogs left off snapping at the flies clustered on their mangy ears and sores, and rushed to bark at the mourners. The din rose to the sky; and vultures took flight from the trees to float a hundred drifting shadows over the rooftops. It was too much! Yet the noise still swelled and grew. The whole courtyard was knee-deep in prostrate wailing women, with a horde of onlookers crowding in, a baying pack of mongrels, and a cloud of vultures overhead. It was all too much, and inevitably brought on the sirocco, that arose in the shape of one of those swift and violent whirlwinds of dust and kapok that the Horodugu dry season alone can produce. The wind toppled, snatched and blinded, and the din stopped as dogs and mourners ran to take shelter in and around the huts. The vultures were scattered to the far horizons. Fama struggled, like a master boatman in a storm, with the wild flapping of his wind-bellied robe. A few moments later the whirlwind had vanished, and the mourners rushed to start up again. 'No, no! God in his Book has forbidden weeping for the dead.' No more howling! No more wailing! Cousin Lasina had lived and died as a true Muslim. And there was no point! Really none! On the ancestors' head! It was a distressed, weary, meditative Fama who received the traditional token of welcome, a calabash of cool water.

'Thank you all! Thank you! God reward you all,' he groaned, before lifting it to his lips.

7　Swarms of lizards and vultures tore open his ribs; he survived thanks to Balla's wisdom

Had it not been for Malinke duplicity, the first night would have been restful, like a shady stream at the end of a long journey on foot during the harmattan season. But the falseness! Malinke are full of duplicity because deep down inside they are blacker than their skin, while the words they speak are whiter than their teeth. Are they fetish-worshippers or Muslims? A Muslim heeds the Koran, a fetish-worshipper follows the Koma; but in Togobala, everyone publicly proclaims himself a devout Muslim, but everyone privately fears the fetish. Neither lizard nor swallow!

Once the keening women had been silenced, it was time for Fama to be shown to his quarters. The Koran says that once dead, summoned by God, a man has departed this earth forever; and Malinke custom assigns the head of a family his own patriarchal hut within the compound. No doubt about it then. There was the spacious hut left empty since Cousin Lasina's death, that had housed all the great Dumbuya ancestors. Fama need only open it up and settle in. But among the Bambara, the unbelievers, the Kaffirs, one must never sleep in a dead man's room without performing a small sacrifice to ward off spirits and shades. The fetish-priest and sorcerer Balla, the village unbeliever (we'll have more to say about him later on, the wily old beast, the old hyena) reminded Fama of this infidel's custom. In spite of his deep faith in the Koran, in God and in Mohammed, Fama spent the whole night in a little hut, huddled between some old water-jars and a mangy mongrel. A most unpleasant night! It had to be that way. Nothing is good or evil in itself. It is speech that turns a thing into good or evil. And misfortune always, inevitably, follows the transgression of a custom, if the culprit was warned that such a custom existed, especially in the case of the customs of a village in the bush.

In Togobala, everyone is impatient for morning, as if the dark of night were a dangerous prison, and the light of day meant freedom and peace. Awake before cock's crow, Fama was able to wash, dress with care, pray, tell his beads at leisure, vigourously clean his teeth and establish himself in front of the patriarchal hut in the manner befitting the legitimate descendant of the Dumbuya dynasty, as if he had slept there. The praise-singer Jamuru sat on his right, the dog squeezed in under the princely chair, and other attendants settled on mats spread in a semi-circle at his feet; they were awaiting the successive waves of callers to come.

A harmattan dawn always lasts a long time, because of the lingering cold and mist; it is a peaceful time, too, with no one stirring in the village except for a few boys, their dogs at their heels, setting out to dig up rat-holes, and two or three women going back and forth from the creek with gourds on their heads. Nothing but mist. Jamuru the praise-singer was in a lively mood, and had a great deal to say. Fama did not listen to him; his thoughts were elsewhere.

Morning was turning things bright, revealing them anew. Fama gazed untiringly at the compound, taking stock. As an inheritance, there wasn't much substance to it. Even a legless chicken could easily do the rounds. Eight huts still standing, just that, their walls cracked from roof to ground, their fire-blackened thatch at least five years old. A lot there to plaster and roof before the rains really started. The stable across the way was empty, and the great hut where horses had been tethered had by now forgotten even the smell of horse-piss. Between the two stood the small hut for goats, that now contained all in all: three billy-goats, two nanny-goats and a kid, scrawny and smelly, intended as offerings to Balla's fetishes. As for human beings, there weren't many able-bodied workers. Four men, two of them old, and nine women, seven of them old women who had somehow managed to avoid dying. Two men to do the farming! Never in life have two men ever been able to grow enough to fill fourteen bellies, rainy season and dry! And the taxes, party dues and all the other cursed cash payments required since Independence, where were they to come from? Truly, there was nothing real, solid or enduring here for Fama to rely on...

*   *   *

'Tell me, Jamuru, my faithful one, how do heads of households manage here?'

'Master! Ah, master!' The old praise-singer began by gathering his robe about him. 'But, master! I wanted to tell you all about that. You haven't been listening. No callers yet? Good! There's still time for me to explain it all. The only, only people who have survived colonialism, independence, the single party, socialism and self-help are the old men, heads of households, who have secrets. Take me, for instance, master; me, Jamuru, descendant of the praise-singers favoured by the Dumbuya family; do you know my secret?

'Tomassini, that was the name of the first *commandant de cercle* here. His taste in African women (he had his reasons) was for raw firm-fleshed virgins like the first green mangoes of the rainy season. Matali! Ah! my dear daughter Matali! may God grant you boundless success and prosperity. When Matali leapt in among the dancers, the drumming, the singing, the earth all vibrated to the rhythm of her hips and breasts, her swaying buttocks rustling with a hundred strings of beads. Like an antelope she bounded, and landed at Tomassini's feet. He whistled admiringly. "Nice!" That was it, her fate was sealed. That very evening, Matali was led to the *commandant*'s camp. Things went wrong when the time came to tear off her loincloth. Well, what could you expect; in those days girls were properly brought up. She refused, struggled, fought her way past guards and through doors, and disappeared into the bush. She was more vigorous than a two-year-old heifer, and what a beauty! what a beauty! The *commandant* hadn't seen anything to beat her in all Horodugu. Her skin! Black, a glossy black like the quill-feathers of the creek-bird, white even teeth that looked as if they weren't meant for eating, a fine straight nose like a taut thread, breasts like yams, firm and gleaming, and the voice of a blackbird. Even after his return to headquarters, the white man was still obsessed with her. He gave orders. Matali was brought to him under heavy guard. He made her pregnant, twice: two boys, one right after the other.

'While those little mulattoes were growing up, moving from one school to another and from one city to the next, Dakar, Gorée and so on, their mother, my daughter Matali, continued to do well for herself, built herself a compound and some shops; so she grew rich, still courted by the European bachelors posted to the district, for she remained beautiful. Finally, remembering her father's precepts and the injunctions of the Koran, she married the Fulani interpreter, who although he had twelve wives made her his favourite.

'What I can swear', the praise-singer shifted his chair slightly, 'what I can swear is that never, not once, not for a single day did Matali forget her parents. The colonial period went by me like a breeze: the father of the *commandant*'s woman was always a special case. Come dearth or plenty, rainy season or dry, Matali has never failed me, not even in these difficult times of Independence and the single party. Do you know what has become of my two little mulatto grandsons? One is governor of a province, secretary-general, deputy and mayor; the other is a doctor, ambassador, and director of something-or-other the name of which I can never remember. They too never forget their grandfather, nor their mother. Praise be to God! Honour and good fortune to Matali! It's thanks to them that I'm alive.'

Indeed the old praise-singer looked as though he had been carefully preserved and dried; all white-haired and serene, glowing as few people do in Horodugu; thin, but with the healthy thinness of old age; with a shaven skull, a few wrinkles at the nape of his neck, below his cheek-bones and on his forehead; shining eyes set between lashes, eyebrows and whiskers as white as a cattle egret's down. His speech was fluent, his intelligence sparkling. His was the serenity God reserves for a few old men among the staunchest believers, the elect. A praise-singer, a man of caste, whereas Fama's cousin...

'Let me tell you about your cousin, master; truly he had a hard time of it with Independence. Let me tell you...'

Too late; the mist had fled the village, and groups of callers were arriving on all sides.

'*Humba! Humba!*'

'May God reward you!'

'Those are the Sise. Their compound is on the path that leads to the creek. One of the late Dumbuya's wives was a Sise.'

The praise-singer identified the callers.

'*Humba! Humba!*'

'May God rain blessings upon you!'

'The Keita. You may remember, Fama, that a cousin of yours is married to a Keita.'

The Kuyate, the Konate, the Jabata were all related to him in some way. The ancestors of all these families had settled in the area during the rule of such-and-such a Dumbuya. Jamuru the praise-singer knew all these things, and expounded them at length.

And Fama sat there, enthroned, haughty. He scarcely looked at the callers. His eyelids would close, as befitted a true panther totem, and the *Humba*! would burst out. In this harmattan dawn before the Dumbuya palace, for a moment, just for a moment, the world as it should be soared anew. Callers thronged. Fama held sway as if beggary, marriage to a barren woman, bastard Independence, all his past life and present worries had never existed. The praise-singer's words flowed on like bird-song. Callers came and went.

Suddenly, a stench like a civet-cat's arse: Balla, the old freedman, had arrived. He was big and fat, bulging like a queen termite from a tight hunter's jerkin, and blind, with shaky steps like those of a two-day-old puppy. He was led to sit on Fama's right. Flies swarmed in his plaited, amulet-laden hair, and in his eye-sockets, his nose, his ears. The old man slowly raised his elephant-tail fan, and at a stroke swatted them in clusters. Flies littered the ground.

He, Balla, was not a caller, an outsider, but one of the Dumbuya family, a former slave who had remained with his masters after emancipation. People reproached him for being late. He did not hear them. They raised their voices. He caught the words, chewed them over slowly; his cheeks widened (that was a smile) and he began to speak, first calmly and slowly, then faster and faster, louder and louder, until he nearly choked. Late ... Uh! if Balla was late, it was because he had done his work, consulted and worshipped the fetishes, then made several sacrificial offerings on Fama's behalf, to make the ancestral home safe to dwell in, to ward off bad luck and evil spells during his stay. Then he had anointed his legs, feet, neck, head and shoulders with a paste of kaolin and votive saliva.

'I'm all over pains; lucky I'm an old beast, an old hound, an old hyena! Uh! Uh! Uh!...'

The last callers had left. Everyone was looking at the old freedman, grotesque but feared, and mocking him; except the praise-singer Jamuru, who was annoyed by the whole business and sometimes said just what he thought of it. An out-and-out heathen like Balla, in a good Muslim village like Togobala! A fetish-worshipper, a caster of evil spells, a public enemy of God! A disgrace!

'They say that Balla is going to burn his fetishes, convert and bow down in prayer,' insinuated one of the company.

'Lies! Lies!' growled the old freedman. 'Lies! Ayo! Ayo! I'm the oldest man alive in the whole province. Don't you think it's because I've no dealings with God, that God has forgotten about me? Uh! Uh! Uh! Uh!'

Everyone burst out laughing; even Fama smiled briefly. Jamuru fumed with annoyance.

Yet Balla and Jamuru had to put up with each other. They were equals. They alone in Horodugu (in the world, they claimed) had lived through Samory's wars, European rule and Independence. Both of them, the praise-singer and the freed slave, were old and faithful servants of the Dumbuya; both had witnessed the great days of the great Dumbuya, and both had seen the dynasty dry up and dwindle away until its only hope was one rather sterile man. Both of them feared – the fear was like a clenched fist in their hearts – that the Dumbuya dynasty might die out and disappear. Jamuru had survived famine, war and the present régime (praise be to the All-Powerful) thanks to Matali. May God reward her a hundred-fold! Balla the infidel, the heathen, believed himself to be immortal like a baobab tree, and swore that he would outlive Independence. An evil power, like a challenge to the fetish, cannot last long. He had always refused to taste conversion, and he had done well. A fetishist among Muslim Malinke, he had become wealthy, feared and well-fed above all others. You know what they're like: the Malinke are full of wickedness, and God grows weary of satisfying their malevolence; they suffer many misfortunes, and God grows weary of assisting them. Then, when God turns aside or fails to relieve him, a Malinke runs to the fetish, runs to Balla. The fetish strikes, even kills at times. And Balla's malevolent client pays, and performs sacrifices to the fetish; so does the victim, or his heirs, in order to contain the destructive power of the evil spell cast upon the family. Both parties pay. This side or the other of the creek, the grass was always green for Balla. Come misfortune, dispelled or not, come illness, healed or not, they always pay; they always sacrifice a chicken or a goat. In other words, whichever way things turned out, Balla always benefited. That was his secret. That was how the big, fat old beast had survived and endured.

Lies! Lies! Balla asserted. A great hunter, one who knows animals, things, medicines and incantations, who worships the fetishes and spirits, doesn't die off like a day-old chick. Colonial rule, illness, famine, even Independence only strike those whose *ni* and *ja*, whose soul and spirit double are empty and weak because they haven't respected their totem.

77

The old man's chief worry was not his impending death, but the decrepitude and decay of the Dumbuya dynasty; he and Jamuru agreed there. Independence had suppressed the chiefdom, dethroned Fama's cousin, and set up a committee in the village, with a president. A sacrilege, a disgrace! Togobala belonged to the Dumbuya. In the twilight of their days, the two old men were striving to reinstate the chiefdom and restore the world to its rightful state. Unfortunately, in Africa these days Togobala, the Dumbuya and even Horodugu were of less account than one grain in a sack of millet. They believed in it, however, and were actively employing themselves. Jamuru had already dug into his secret caches, brought out his wealth, distributed kola-nuts among the callers on Fama's behalf. Balla had tethered goats and cattle behind the village for the funeral ceremonies. The Dumbuya weren't finished; it was Independence, single parties and presidents that would go up in smoke. The cousin had left two wives as prolific as mice; Fama could beget numerous male Dumbuya (Balla had a medicine for that!). Fama must take care, though, not to mingle words with the committee people, nor to tread in their footsteps. They were enemies, accursed. If need be, Balla would unsheath his fetish and strike dead anyone who stood in the way; and Jamuru would plead his cause with the governor.

Thus, in the quest to regain power Fama could rely on a fetish-priest, a praise-singer, money and political support; in other words, the ultimate devotion of two old men on their last legs. That was something, but not everything. What was lacking was this: the prince himself didn't believe in it, and who could say whether, deep down, he even wished it?

The sun was sinking in the sky, its glare softening. The hour of third prayer was near; today, Fama was to say third prayer at the grave-side. To visit the deceased's final resting-place is – who can doubt it? – as important a ceremony as the funeral rite.

Temper! It was a bad-tempered Fama: sour-eyed, knotty-browed, tight-lipped, who set out for the cemetery. Since daybreak, the two old men had been deliberately flattering and irritating him. Not one of the incredible, the innumerable bastard deeds of Independence and the one-party system did they leave unmentioned, the insults, injustices, breaches of custom and challenges to the Dumbuya. And that was not all; just when they were about to leave, yet another palaver began. Balla wanted to go with them. A blind man – what could he see? Nothing. An old man with swollen aching legs – when would they arrive there with him along? Perhaps at sunset. A Kaffir whose forehead never touched the ground – what would he do there? Nothing and nothing. They thought he was joking. But no! Balla insisted. He evoked the duty to pay a last visit to the deceased. As the palaver was flaring up again, Fama angrily quenched it with a gesture of his right hand. Balla was not coming.

The cemetery began just beyond the last huts of the village, beyond the rubbish dump, east of the village on the slope of a low laterite hill. They walked in silence, Fama and a marabout in the lead, between two courtyards and across a compound, and left the village, passing near the great mango-tree with leafy drooping branches; Fama's father's funeral procession had taken the same route, but that had been in the middle of the rains, in weak sunlight reflected by the seasonal clouds and surging greenery. Now, the dry season was at its height. Bush-fires and the dry harmattan wind had laid everything bare; even the little clump of trees in the middle of the cemetery. Poor little clump of trees, its mystery dispelled! When Fama was a child it had seemed deep and vast as a forest, haunted by devils, ghosts and spirits! They clambered over graves hyenas had emptied of their dead, sometimes even gathering up their robes and shedding their slippers to leap over them. The cousin's grave was a red hummock of freshly dug laterite, with a paraffin lamp set at each end. Why the lamps, and the branches? The grave-robbing hyenas of Horodugu are voracious, greedy for dead bodies. They have to be kept away for the first ten nights. Luckily they're as timorous as a turtle's head; a lit lamp and the rustle of leaves in the night wind will make them flee in terror, leaving a trail of steaming droppings.

'Thank you! Thank you all! May God's blessings reward those who have shown such care and humanity!'

Fama's voice cracked with emotion. He gathered together the folds of his robe, and squatted along with the others, just behind the marabout at the head of the procession, one step west of the grave. The prayer began.

The marabout grunted an emphatic '*bissimilahi*', stumbled over the title of the surat to be recited seventeen times, rasped out the name of the verse to be said seven times. And a solemn, mysterious wind, sun and universe descended upon them. A light wind wafted the burnt smell of the savanna, with sudden gusts of an unbearable stench, and rustled among the leaves of the branches laid on the grave. The sun caressed the backs of their bowed heads, and its radiance seemed to magnify their murmur, sparkling among the graves and fallen leaves. It was the whisper of the shades and doubles of the buried dead, emerging from the other world to sit and drink in their prayers.

A vast invisible throng gathered about the men in prayer. Among them were all the noble and valiant Dumbuya ancestors. What a sorry figure Fama must seem to them! Their only male descendant, plucked naked and bled dry by the colonial era and by Independence. It was there, and in no other place than this very graveyard, that the Dumbuya dynasty would end. But would it end with Fama? Fama imagined himself dead, without difficulty; without fear he could see his double, his *ja* emerging from his body to take its place among the shades and judge him with mercy. The Fama squatting there in his white robe was a man upon whom weighed great responsibilities; his duty was to prolong the dynasty, to make Togobala and all Horodugu prosper. Fate, destiny, fortune, and the blessings, will and last judgement of God all descended upon him, obscuring and contradicting each other. Destiny seemed a preordained path, and Fama a blade of grass swept along in the flood of a great river. The proof? The times without number he had eluded, challenged and overcome death, that will finish him off whenever destiny wills it. Everything bears both death and life. Rain brings down lightning and life-giving water, earth brings forth harvest and entombs the dead, the sun spreads light and drought; the years bring on age and famine, children and Independence.

Fama realized that he had lost count of the surats and verses. He stopped chanting. A stronger wind was blowing now, and the stench was worse. Fama wondered briefly what it was that stank so foully, then sank once more into his thoughts.

A fate as hard as iron, as heavy as a mountain, may yet be warded off with sacrifices, with the help of the dead. Ancestors! You great Dumbuya! I will slaughter sacrifices for you, but all of you, if such be God's will, dispel unlawfulness and sterility, kill off Independence and the one-party system, epidemics and locust swarms! Just then, the marabout breathed out a loud '*alfatia*'. All those praying held out cupped hands, to receive the blessing and lift it to their foreheads. Many wishes that the other world might be favourable to the dead man. The prayer was over.

'Where are the graves of my father and my dear mother?' asked Fama.

The praise-singer guided him to his father's grave, and they stood there. Bush-fires had spared the grass growing there in the hollow. Jamuru and Fama prayed; just as they bent down to tidy the grave, a lizard scurried from between their feet and vanished through a hole in the side of the tomb. Startled, Fama stood up.

'Death is the great challenge!' murmured the praise-singer.

They neatened the caved-in tomb, with its cracks where rats and lizards dwelt. His mother's grave was over near the central clump of trees. A few paces away their hearts leapt in sudden shock. Vultures took flight or ran off. Horror! In the midst of a throat-searing stench and a cloud of flies, lay a dead dog, eyes and nose torn away. They prayed at the foot of the grave, in spite of the pestilential smell, as strong as if they had been trapped inside the dog's entrails. The vultures, reassured by their silence, waddled towards the beast. The prayer was a short one! All together they left the cemetery, deeply moved. All except the old praise-singer, who was talking, because he wanted to take advantage of Balla's absence to urge his master to hold fast to Islam, to warn him against the fetish-priest's heathen practices and the lies of the people in the committee and the party. Fama heard nothing.

Before them, behind the silk-cotton tree, the dying sun was caught in a swamp of purple. Dozens of vultures, awakened, were taking flight from the trees, lured by the aroma of the dead dog. The village was full of evening life, as everything made ready for night: the last burst of twittering from the weaver-birds in the tamarind trees, the children shouting and dogs barking after the goats, to bring them home before the wild beasts came out; the hunters, rat-catchers and wood-gatherers back from the fields, and the last dying breath of a harmattan day, that searches the furthest recesses of your heart and stirs up the drums of memory, thoughts of childhood, of great moments, of history's sudden changes and the uncertainty of the future. Suddenly the call to fourth prayer rang out. A sun had run its course.

The night was spent without danger in the dead man's bed; the shades had been placated by sacrifice. When the hooting of owls, the howls of hyenas filled a night already peopled with spirits, Fama became anxious and his mind began to roam. It wandered among empty graves, chased lizards and vultures, stumbled over dead dogs and fled before spirit doubles before finally dissolving, breathless, into sleep and the night. He slept soundly.

Shortly before cock's crow he started awake, troubled by the vision of a hideous nightmare. Dogs with eyes, ears and nose torn away were chasing swarms of lizards and vultures, that were tearing open his ribs and loins to seek refuge there. Once his fear had abated, he scrupulously recited the surats that ward off spirits in the night.

In the morning, he confided in Balla, who already knew about the nightmare. Fama's *ja*, his double, had left his body while he was asleep and had been chased by the double-devouring sorcerers.

'Fama, believe me! you enemies don't sleep! In the night I heard and followed flights of sorcerers aiming for your hut. I scattered them and made them flee with incantations.'

So Fama could live without fear, so long as his freedman Balla drew breath. But he must offer sacrifices to the shades of the ancestors. Koranic prayers, even Paradise cannot contain the Malinke dead, especially the great Dumbuya. Their *ja*, their doubles are vigorous and untameable. Sacrifices and much blood; sacrifices are beneficial, always and everywhere.

8 The suns sounding the dry season and Fama, his nights bristling with bedbugs and Mariam, were all trapped; but the bastards did not win

Already five suns set. There were eighteen left to see rise before Cousin Lasina's fortieth-day funeral rites.

The dry-season days, like the eggs of one guinea-fowl, emerged and dropped each exactly like the others. The same mornings with the same kapok mist and the same scent of pissed-on embers, the same evenings when the dust-laden winds died down and it was the earth's turn to sigh. First morning.

Day began at first cock's crow. The moon was drowning in the low sky (it was in its last quarter). The muezzin called out the summons to first prayer, then wandered through the narrow alley-ways, chanting verses and occasionally stopping.

'You! I'm talking to you!' he would roar from behind the wall in the cottony morning mist.' 'Stop holding her, turning her, and telling that woman lies. Arise and pray, reflect and compare! The Almighty, the final call, the Day of Judgement, Hell, the unending pain and terror of hell-fire. And God's call comes without warning! Prayer is the only provision for the journey into eternity. Arise and salute your Lord!'

This muezzin, clearly malevolent, would roar thus every morning behind Fama's hut, although there was no need. Fama was not sleeping with any woman, and he was ready, washed and dressed before the call to prayer. At the mosque he prayed at length, and spent too much time telling his beads, at least in Balla's opinion.

He met his praise-singer Jamuru there, and together in the early morning they visited each compound in turn, to greet its inhabitants and ask if they had spent the night in peace. Then they established themselves in front of the ancestral home of the Dumbuya, and chewing-stick in mouth received the greetings of their morning callers.

And the dry-season morning, like any mother, began very painfully to give birth to the enormous harmattan sun. Truly painfully; that was because of Balla's fetishes. The fetish-priest swore that the sun would not shine on the village so long as his fetishes were out of doors. He woke late in the morning, and would take them all out to sacrifice a red cock to them; so the sun was held back for a long time, caught in a tangle of mist, smoke and clouds. Once Balla's fetishes were put away, the sun could break free, having by that time reached the top of the mango-tree near the cemetery. All of a sudden it burst forth; and after the free radiant sun, like chicks after a mother hen, came all the harmattan's children.

It began with the whirlwinds full of dust and dead leaves that blew down from the cemetery, alive with spirits and the shades of the dead. A true curse! They rushed through the village, tearing thatch from roofs, sending calabashes spinning, snatching up clothes, then roared off through the bush. The sky rose blue and high, so high that the highest-soaring vultures could no longer touch it. Everything enchanted Fama, for in his heart rose memories of the good harmattans of his childhood.

'Truly, a very good dry season,' he murmured.

'No,' protested Balla, who had finally joined the assembly. 'No! this is a miserable puny wretch of a harmattan. The great dry seasons, the real ones are gone for good along with the great hunts. Uh! Uh! ... Remember, master, when you were young. I was still hunting ...'

And the palaver would take up Balla's hunting stories. Jamuru knew them all, and could tell them better than the old fetish-priest himself.

How did Balla become the greatest hunter of all Horodugu?

At the hour of *urebi*, far out in the unexplored bush, at the foot of a hill where a cool spring flowed, he met or rather there appeared to him a spirit. It was a spirit of the hunt. All Malinke have heard tell of such spirits, that live off warm blood and are especially fond of human blood, that lead wild animals as shepherds lead their flocks. This spirit was naked, as tall as Balla, its head shaved except for a thick plait of hair down the middle, hanging long and low as a lizard's tail, and of course, swinging from its left hand, a spirit gun, no longer than a man's arm, with a golden barrel: the kind of gun the lone hunter can hear booming in the distant bush, in the midst of the dry season.

'I have brought you here to propose a pact,' said the spirit.

Without haste, without the least fear (had he not himself made sacrifices to bring about this meeting!) Balla calmly answered: 'What sort of pact?'

The spirit explained. Indeed, Balla knew all the conditions: spirits of the hunt always offer the same pact. Every time the hunter came out, the spirit would lead him far into the bush; there, the spirit would gather wild animals as a shepherd does his flock, and Balla would shoot as many as he liked. But one far-off day, instead of leading Balla it would slaughter him, and gorge on his warm blood.

'But what day?' asked Balla. The spirit did not answer. They never specify the day.

Once the pact was made, the spirit and Balla had scoured the bush together for years and years, as inseparable as index and middle finger. Every dry season Balla heaped exploit upon exploit, like a farmer lining up ridges of soil. Balla liked to tell about them, and from one end of a broad sun to the other, without ever repeating himself (and with Jamuru's corrections and comments) he would bore the assembly to death with his hunting stories. For instance: his triumphant exploit at Fama's father's funeral. Let us tell it right away.

The drumming was in full spin, and it was the hunters' turn to dance. All the hunters of Horodugu were there, hunters of every hide and hair, even hunters who had seven tigers to their name. The walls and ground shook with rifle volleys, and there was so much smoke that it looked as if the village were on fire. All kinds of promises were made: a tiger, a lion, and elephant, but in due course ... That is to say, next dry season, next rainy season. Balla leapt in among the dancers, bounded into the air, and fired the four fingers' breadth of powder packed into the barrel of his gun. The boom! Balla asked all the women of the village to put pots of sauce on the fire, and disappeared into the bush. A while later, when the drums were still beating and the pots had not yet come to the boil, he returned with the tail of a black buffalo. People went to look for the beast. In the thickets! the nearby thickets where villagers relieved themselves and goats grazed, Balla had shot a black buffalo, one of those solitary, impetuous buffalo that usually roam the remote bush, their horns laden with nests, followed by a flock of swallows. The greatest hunters there had to swallow their guns and trophies.

While we're on the subject of buffalo, Balla once had an epic fight with a spirit-buffalo. In the distant plains of the Bafing river, Balla fired his four fingers' breadth of powder between the horns of a buffalo. To his amazement the beast charged him, as if that shot had had no more force to it than a grandmother's fart. A wise and experienced hunter, Balla understood right away that he had attacked a spirit-buffalo, and would have to draw on his deepest knowledge. It was a single combat between the man of knowledge and the spirit-animal! The man uttered an incantation that set his gun floating at tree-level, between earth and sky; another incantation, and Balla was sitting on his gun as comfortably as in a hammock, too high for the buffalo to reach him. But the buffalo was as cunning as the man; the beast changed into an eagle and hooked its claws into Balla, who escaped only by another spell that turned him into a needle; but the buffalo, still pursuing him, became a thread and the thread glided swiftly towards the needle's eye. To escape the thread, Balla quickly changed from the needle into a twig, and the twig vanished in the long grass. Still in pursuit, the buffalo turned into a flame, the flame began to burn the bush, smoke rose from the fire, the fire's crackling made a deafening noise, and the whole bush was in turmoil. Under cover of this turmoil, Balla took the beast by surprise with a final spell, a masterly metamorphosis. Our hunter turned into a river, and the river drowned the flame, extinguishing the animal's *ja*, its vital substance; it lost its magic powers, turned back into a buffalo, snorted angrily, toppled over and died. Once more, Balla had been the wisest; he emerged at once from the river, that dried up, pulled out his knife and cut off the beast's tail. He examined the buffalo: it had two gold rings through its muzzle. It must have been the favourite buffalo of a prince among the forest spirits, the gold rings being used to tether it.

Then one after the other many years passed, years of happiness, of unhappiness, of famine, of epidemics, of drought: the hunting, like the Joliba river, never ran dry. Whenever he went out into the bush, Balla's heart pounded and his belly heaved, for this time might well be the last. Balla tried to learn the spirit's fate. A spirit is like a man, and for every individual there is a thing that will extinguish the life in his body, like water poured upon embers; this thing cuts short our destiny: it is our *kala*. For three years Balla consulted marabouts, fetishes, sorcerers, and killed sacrifice upon sacrifice, to discover the *kala* of this spirit of the hunt. One Monday the spirit came to meet him just outside the village. They walked in the still of evening until they came to a creek, that the spirit crossed ahead of its companion. From the other bank, Balla fired four fingers' breadth of powder at its back. The spirit howled and fell. The blood and howling burst into flames and set light to the bush. Balla walked back to the village and hung his gun and gear up on the wall, for good. His hunting days were over; this piece of treachery meant that as long as he lived, he could never again set foot in the bush. Do you know what the spirit's *kala* was? The droppings of a musk-deer! On top of his four fingers of powder, Balla had placed three musk-deer droppings. That was what killed the spirit of the hunt.

The hunting stories made the days pass easily. The sun rose quickly overhead, and all sat round the communal calabashes for the midday meal. Then, before their hands were dry, the sun reached the hour of second prayer. The palaverers all lined up to pray, all except Balla. The fetish-priest was kept busy killing fleas by crushing the seams of his garment between his teeth, and slaughtering flies with his fan, while the others earned priceless divine blessings with their prayers.

Then the hunting stories began again. The sun sank to the hour of third prayer, and once more the sheepskins were shaken and spread. At fourth prayer, the sun was setting. A dry season twilight!

Fama's nights were often long. The ancestral home, the royal dwelling-place of Horodugu, was one of the oldest, and therefore housed the oldest, largest, reddest rats, fleas and cockroaches. They swarmed about him as he lay, and sleep and Fama parted company. In his wakeful head and heart, worries blew like whirlwinds.

First came the money worries. Togobala, need it be repeated, was poorer than an orphan's one pair of drawers, as dry as the river Tuko in the middle of the harmattan, tormented by hunger and thirst. What little money Fama had brought with him had vanished more quickly than the morning dew. There were meals and sacrifices to be paid for. Every day the circle seated round the calabashes of *toh* had grown wider, as age-mates chose mealtimes to come and greet him. Then there were the praise-singers (except Jamuru), the joking relations who made demands, and all the others who moaned and stretched out their hands; Fama had to give, he had to be generous, and was, so much so that he was about to give away his underclothes when the two old servants of the dynasty, the old praise-singer and the old freedman, came to his rescue.

They were almost compelled to. In Togobala, poverty could neither be healed nor hidden. With empty hands and pockets, Fama was short-tempered and irritable. He frowned whenever anyone approached him, and became furious when he had to give. All day long he was as intractable as a newly circumcised donkey. To do away with this bad temper, and stop the palavers being spoilt by outbursts of rage, of their own accord the two men paid for him. And Fama let them.

In broad daylight, right in the middle of Togobala, the last of the Dumbuya had become his servants' parasite. It was pitiful, disgraceful, unbelievable! But when Fama lay alone throughout the long sleepless nights, he found it shamefully soothing. He had no more money worries.

Even without money worries, the nights remained long, clammy, prickly with bites and stings, because Fama spent them alone, all alone, without a woman. That is to say that he sometimes twisted and turned, clamped his thighs together, groaned even, his mind and heart entangled in women's matters, or – let us speak frankly – the matter of Mariam.

Mariam's cloths, her head-ties, her merriment, her talk were forever appearing and reappearing in his nightly thoughts and dreams. He was waiting for her. Mariam! At first sight the young widow had stung Fama into a writhing torment that had seized him only once before, when as a young boy just entering puberty he had caught a glimpse of a young wife of his father's completely naked. He felt completely transformed, aroused to a mule-like virility.

It all began the very evening of Fama's arrival in Togobala. He had gone to call on the widows, and bent down to lean through the door of the hut where they sat in mourning (they would remain cloistered for forty days). Mariam sat carding at the back of the hut, near the door opposite, so that the setting sun shone full upon her in her mourning attire, that – one should not say so – suited her marvellously, like antimony round a monkey's eyes.

'Thank you, women! Take heart! Yours is the pain! Yours is

the sorrow!' had exclaimed Fama and the praise-singer Jamuru who was with him.

At once the three widows and the old women their companions had flung themselves into weeping and wailing. Fama could not have his fill of gazing at Mariam; she seemed to him to have decked herself in mourning as a courted girl decks herself in a gold necklace for a dance. You could have sworn to God she was pretending to weep, wailing for the fun of it. None of it sank any deeper than the tip of her lashes, the pout of her lips. Her hair, left unplaited according to custom and tangled like a madwoman's, lent sly allure to her shining squirrel's eyes. Her face and throat glowed, and her breasts, bound tight in the indigo-dye cloth, jutted round and firm as a young girl's. Her hips and thighs spread ample and billowy beneath the cloth. What a thrill it would be to touch her!

'Enough! enough weeping! Every death is God's will!' cried the praise-singer. 'Tears will not raise the dead.'

They still moaned, but more softly.

'Jamuru, speak to your master,' begged Mariam in an affected tone of voice. 'Tell him that we rely on him alone, he is our father and mother.'

Fama had looked at the young woman while she was speaking, but had at once lowered his gaze for fear of giving cause for scandal; she had flashed a coquettish smile at him!

'Have no fear, all of you! Fama can be relied on,' the praise-singer had said.

Every morning after leaving the mosque, Jamuru and Fama would stop at the widow's door to greet them. Mariam would be waiting for them. Let us say it, for God loves the truth! She was beautiful, bewitching, just the woman to keep an aging man like Fama warm for the remainder of his days. If she were set alongside Salimata, the latter would not be worth half a kola-nut. Indeed Fama now rarely thought of his wife in the city, and had not even sent her a word of greeting since arriving in Togobala. Besides, Mariam belonged to Fama, she was the part of the inheritance worth having.

'In spite of her shocking bad temper, master, don't let a lively fish like Mariam escape your net,' advised Jamuru, and he continued:

‾ 'That young woman's many faults tormented the deceased during the last years of his life. She'll lie you blind and toothless, and steal you hollow.'

Maliciously, the praise-singer lowered his voice, and looked about him:

'She has a smile for every youth, and can't say no to an advance. And the young men of the village, the shameless young men of Independence, have no respect, none of them, even for sacred things like the young wives of old men.'

'No! there's no harm, there's no fault without a remedy. Uh! Uh!' muttered Balla the fetish-priest.

Let nothing turn a man aside in his quest for a fruitful woman, a woman who absorbs, preserves and nourishes, nothing! And Mariam was a woman with a sound belly, a belly that could carry twelve pregnancies. Balla could tell, before he went blind, by the young woman's way of walking. As for unfaithfulness, Uh! Uh! decent women were as rare now in Horodugu as rams with one testicle. Balla could swear to that. If you ask a woman who's only slept with her husband to step over a dying horse, if she doesn't do it quickly the beast will lift her as it rises. The other day when Balla had a prostrate mare to treat, he had three married women step over her, mothers of several children, and the beast collapsed and died that very night. Nevertheless, adultery must be repressed. Balla would make young men keep their hands off Mariam. He would attach a powerful fetish to her. At best, the man who mounted her wouldn't be able to withdraw, and he'd stay trapped in her vulva until Balla pronounced the counter-fetish; otherwise, after he'd made love his penis would shrink and disappear into his lower belly. And that would be the end of him. To be called a woman-chaser you need something that stands up in front. Uh! Uh! Uh! . . .

So he had taken her. Mariam would be his thing. Every night Fama thought of her, imagined himself turning her, caressing her, spreading her, once the period of mourning was over. Every night except – need it be said? – the two nights before the great palaver: a Monday and a Tuesday.

On Monday morning Jamuru had drawn him aside, and leaned over to spit the secret in his ear. The village and committee president (his name was Babu) and all the other committee members were going to question Fama; not for a joke either, nor to honour him! There would be one-party system in the sauce, and *sous-préfet*, and counter-revolution, with still more things Jamuru had forgotten. The palaver would begin on Wednesday, after third prayer.

This all became official when the committee's praise-singer came to announce it, just when they were about to gather round calabashes full of *toh*, and washed his hands to join their circle.

Sous-préfet, counter-revolution, reaction – all this was extremely serious! For two nights Fama tossed and turned over various problems, crushing fleas, bedbugs and lice. It was serious, and as awkward as a robe too wide at the neck. What with Independence, the single party, the committee and all the rest, the Malinke were by now giddy with exhaustion. They had had enough. But no one said so, and no one knew what to do about it. In the midst of this seething passivity, arrived Fama. He was heralded as the last Dumbuya, a brave and outspoken man whom the Europeans had robbed of the chiefdom. He had returned from the south to settle in the village and become president of the committee. Thus Jamuru and Balla had decided. Why not, when all Horodugu belonged to him? Besides, Fama could tell all the presidents and secretary-generals that the inhabitants of Togobala were completely worn out. Jamuru and Balla had filled the village with still more insolent words: according to them, their master was preparing to throttle Independence, the single party and all committees.

'There was counter-revolution in Togobala, true reaction!' decided the committee and its president, and they made it known far and wide.

The *sous-préfet*, the secretary-general, the governor, the single party rejoiced (for months there had been no reactionaries to track down) and sprang to arms, ready to destroy the dreadful counter-revolutionary in his lair. They even reconstituted vigilante groups, to spy on Fama. It was a truly uncomfortable and dangerous situation.

But they were all Malinke, and no Malinke ever keeps to one bank of a river. You could shout yourself hoarse abusing reactionaries, then hurriedly put on your slippers to be in time for a meal at Fama's, where seated at the common calabash, between two satisfying peppery mouthfuls, you would regret what you had said in other company, and curse the single party and Independence. Indeed, no one in Togobala bears anyone else a grudge for whatever he may have said in front of the authorities. Colonization, district commissioners, requisitions, epidemics, drought, Independence, the single party and the revolution are all bred of the same dam, all foreign to Horodugu, a kind of curse brought upon them by the devil. Why divide, fight, affront brotherhood and humanity for the sake of such devil's spawn? Others had wielded the whip on behalf of the colonialists. When the Europeans left, they had to face their victims. No more of that.

But why, then? why was everyone preparing for a brutal confrontation, a sort of bullfight? Why was everyone tossing his armful of firewood on to the flames? A Malinke mystery, or the boredom of the long dry-season period of idleness? People would gather up their robes and shed their slippers to take a seat at Fama's palaver. Jamuru and Balla were beside themselves, swearing and abusing the 'committee bastards'. Fama was going to proclaim some home truths, even if the single party were to swallow him alive.

'The president of the committee: the son of a slave. Who ever saw the son of a slave giving orders?'

Thereupon people would quickly return to the committee's palaver, to report what they had heard and listen to what the president had to say:

'Fama! He weighs less than the down round a hen's arse-hole. A good-for-nothing parasite, an empty shell, a sterile carcass., A reactionary, a counter-revolutionary.'

In the name of God! On Tuesday all Togobala (except Balla) spent the whole day (except prayer-times) shifting back and forth between the two palavers. That is why on those two nights, Monday and Tuesday, Fama could not sleep.

On Wednesday the sun reached the hour of third prayer. They prayed together. Half the village had joined Fama's palaver. At last the others arrived: the committee people, with their praise-singer in the lead, then Babu and the eleven other committee members, with the *sous-préfet*'s delegate, followed by the other half of the village. The committee people had come to Fama because he was observing a period of mourning, and in Togobala, since the world began, serious and important matters have always been discussed in the Dumbuya compound. Those who were seated rose, shook hands with the new arrivals, and as good Muslims should, they all inquired after each other's families. That lasted for about as long as it would take a leper to thread a needle. Then people settled on the mats spread outside the huts. Fama, the president Babu and the *sous-préfet*'s delegate were given deck-chairs. The two praise-singers, Jamuru and the committee's man, stood in the middle of the assembly.

The praise-singers spoke first. They introduced the palaver, invoked fraternity, humanism, God and the assiduous quest for truth; in order to assure the population that its dry-season inactivity was going to be enlivened by a high-quality show, they announced that the palaver would last as long as proved necessary, two or three nights even, that the truth might be dug up, pure and bright as a nugget of gold.

The praise-singers called on Babu to speak next. The assembled throng began to hum with murmurs. As soon as he opened his mouth, he showed himself to be a wily, conciliatory son of a slave. The committee president delivered his speech like a man walking on marshy ground, one step at a time, looking about inquiringly and pausing for signs of approval before continuing. He described Fama as a great fighter (Fama himself was startled by this statement). The party stood for the struggle against colonialism, and Fama had defied the Europeans right here in Togobala (had he not been deprived of the chiefdom?) and then in the south. There followed a stream of flattery.

All eyes were on Babu. His face was light-skinned, but dry and lined, with a long nose like a woodpecker's beak, eyes hidden under chimpanzee brows, and projecting ears like sisal leaves – his enemies called him 'big-ears'. He was wearing a faded red fez, its rim greasy and sweat-stained, and a coarse, much-mended cotton robe, and between two proverbs (his speech was full of them) he would plunge his fingers in among his rags to deal with irreverent lice.

Yes, agreed; Fama was peerless and supreme. Yes! Humanism and fraternity are what counts in men's lives. But what next? Babu kept reiterating these two themes, and other commonplaces always respectfully received among Muslim Malinke: divine mercy, the Day of Judgement, truth the staff of righteousness in a palaver. But all of this was introduced with fiery looks, varied intonations, and proverbs, and delivered with more glances, gestures of the head and hands, and proverbs, and the audience joyfully drank it all in. They asked for nothing more: palaver for palaver's sake! Babu the slave's son had conquered the villagers by his eloquence.

Then it was Fama's turn to speak. He did not condescend to utter so much as three words! A Dumbuya – you must admit – could not lower himself to the extent of speaking at any length before a committee made up of sons of slaves. Besides, his praise-singer Jamuru was there; speaking, a praise-singer was in his proper element, like a Dumbuya in warfare, a fish in water or a bird in the sky. He piled phrase upon phrase without pausing for breath, and no phrase was like the one before.

The hour of fourth prayer came all too soon, but everyone prayed scrupulously; then night fell. They parted company, to gather again after fifth prayer. Each brought a blanket, for dry-season nights are cold and windy. Great wood-fires were lit, around which the palaver continued until first cock's crow. They met again on Thursday afternoon, and all evening the voices boomed on before an alert and entertained audience. Fama dozed.

At last the truth burst forth.

The delegate from outside, ignorant of Malinke custom, kept bobbing up to repeat himself over and over, as unconciliating and unmanageable as a mad donkey's erection. What Fama must do – these were his orders, and he wouldn't hear of anything else – was kneel down at the feet of the committee president, touch his lips to the ground, retract all his former words, swear allegiance on the Koran to the party, the committee and the revolution, and swear on the Koran that he would never, secretly or openly, nourish hatred or calumny against the committee and the party. In truth, Fama could no more do all that than he could eat dog-shit.

'Your suggestions,' shouted Jamuru, 'are not compatible with our agreement.'

The delegate's mouth dropped open, as if he had trodden on a viper's tail. He never knew that at the peak of all the hubbub, when things seemed to be moving beyond the villagers' control, the elders had taken fright. If they carried on like this, there would be no more humane feeling, nor brotherhood; no more balance of invisible forces to protect the village; nothing but hatred between families, the spirits' anger, the ancestors' curse. And who would preserve them from drought, locusts, epidemics and famine? They must come to an agreement, to ward off the dangers of discord. Late on Tuesday night, the night before the palaver, the elders summoned Babu and Fama to the cemetery, to appear before the shades of the ancestors. Woe betide whoever reveals what transpired there! The secret council of elders conferred, and evoked the days of old: Fama would remain chief according to custom, and Babu the official president. They also spoke of the future: the suns of Independence and the single party would pass away, as did the suns of Samory and of the Europeans, but there would always be Babu and Dumbuya in Togobala. So they were reconciled.

'Let the palaver run its full course,' they said, 'the villagers like it, and the delegate will be deceived.'

But two days' and two nights' palaver were enough. Jamuru's words were a reminder, a signal.

As soon as he had spoken, all the villagers, exhausted by the palaver, the committee's supporters and the committee members themselves, Fama's supporters and Fama, Jamuru and Balla all knelt down in entreaty. Astonished, the delegate rose. After a moment's silence, he agreed to let Fama become a member of the committee.

All praise to the Almighty! All praise to the shades of the ancestors! So long as the wall does not crack, no cockroach can lodge in it. Cockroaches of Independence, of the single party, of revolution, you will not penetrate, divide and ruin Togobala! Never! Thanks to the sacrifices offered by our ancestors.

Fama felt as pleased as a small bird perched on a twig at sunrise. That night he sank into the deep sleep of a man who has fallen and broken his neck. Without a snore. Fleas, lice, bedbugs and cockroaches swarmed all over him, and even attacked his ears; but in vain. He did not budge until first cock's crow. The bastards had not won in Togobala. Thank you! Thank you all!

9 _After the successful funeral rites came the ill-fated journey_

Why do the Malinke hold funeral rites forty days after a burial? Because exactly forty days after a burial, the dead receive the new-comer into their company, but they will only make him welcome and give him room if they are drunk on blood. Nothing therefore can be more beneficial to the departed than to kill many beasts on the fortieth day. Before the suns of Independence and the suns of the colonial era, the fortieth day of great Malinke would set streams of blood flowing. But now, what with the single party, Independence, poverty, famines and epidemics, at the funeral rites of the greatest men will be killed at most a ram. And what kind of ram? Most likely a half-starved ram, oozing less blood than a carp. And what kind of blood? Blood as thin as the menstrual fluid of a dried-up old maid. That was why Balla was given to saying that the dead of the suns of Independence were all crowded together in the other world, not having been made welcome by their predecessors.

Fama, Balla and Jamuru had decided to ensure a roomy afterlife for the deceased cousin; to that end they renewed the great tradi-tions, and in the Dumbuya courtyard, on the morning of the for-tieth-day funeral rites, they tethered four head of cattle; yes, four! How had they managed?

One young bull had been donated by Balla, the old sorcerer, to honour the Dumbuya and because a sacrifice is never wasted. A cow had been presented by a son-in-law of the deceased; he owed it, because he had not finished paying for his wife when he married her. Finally, two oxen were the cousin's own property. The cattle belonging to the inheritance had been kept hidden; other people wanted to appropriate them at Fama's expense. They did not suc-ceed, because in Togobala the deepest-buried secret always gives off a faint smell; one whisper led to another, and Fama found out a week before the fortieth day that the deceased had entrusted cattle (five head) to a woman who lived in a remote village of southern Horodugu.

'God is great!' he exclaimed, and ordered that two of them be fetched.

Add them up: that made exactly four to be killed. Such a meaty slaughter and feast turned the whole province topsy-turvy; no one wanted to miss it. And all the inhabitants of Horodugu who should (and who should not? after all, the Dumbuya were the chiefs) and could (and who could not, in this off-season?) made ready and set out for Togobala for the fortieth-day funeral rites of the late Lasina, Fama's deceased cousin.

Strangers came from all horizons of the village, Malinke from villages nearby. Nothing was missing on the march: drums, hunters, elders, praise-singers, women, girls and young boys. The bush shook as if trampled by compact herds of elephants. This lasted for one whole sun, from rising to setting, with even a few arrivals during the night, then again all the next morning until noon.

Preparations for the ceremony began after second prayer. Even before then, there were people huddled on mats in the shade of the huts. Little by little the seated throng spread to the neighbouring compound, as far as the cemetery. Then the women arrived, bearing calabashes of cooked food and pots full of sauce, which they lined up near the four tethered cattle. Grain and condiments had been distributed among the village housewives, and since early morning they had been pounding, tending hearth-fires, lifting pots on and off. It was a success: the dishes covered half the little courtyard, and the mingled aromas: *toh*, *futo*, *fonio*, pepper, onion, prompted the general sniffing that precedes great feasts.

The marabouts – prestigious ones! there were even two Al Hadji – squatted in the middle of the courtyard, a step away from the food, and began to shuffle yellowed sheets of paper. Fama was presiding, on the right of the greatest of the marabouts (the tallest one with the largest turban). Jamuru was right behind his master; but Balla had been relegated to the rear, just in front of the brats and dogs, because he was a heathen. Everything was ready for the opening of a great funeral ceremony, worthy of a Dumbuya: four head of cattle in the middle, all shiny and bellowing, countless calabashes and pots of cooked food, and men seated all around as far as the neighbouring courtyards, with the children and a pack of mangy dogs at the far edge.

The head marabout had the praise-singer call for silence, then uttered a loud '*bissimilahi*' and began chanting verses. The few who were privileged to know the text of the Koran, read aloud; most of those present moved closer and listened attentively. But all raised their clasped hands to their foreheads, gleaming in the light of the setting sun; all communed in a single prayer, asking for mercy from God and the shades of the ancestors. How solemn! how dignified! how pious! It was so extraordinary, among Malinke, that the spirits became angry and an evil whirlwind blew down from the cemetery, caught up their robes and the leaves of manuscripts (which in itself did not much matter), rushed at the pots and calabashes, sent a few lids spinning, knocked over a few containers of sauce. Cries of dismay rose from the group at prayer, and many of them, including turbaned marabouts, leapt up to set things right. The whirlwind moved off. But its departure and disappearance far off in the bush, changed nothing. Piety too had departed: people read and prayed with one eye, while the other caressed the cattle and the calabashes full of cooked rice.

To everyone's satisfaction, the head marabout cut short the prayer and called on the praise-singers to speak. They all, even the sorriest of them, made long flowing speeches, for each knew the genealogy and feats of arms of the Dumbuya in Horodugu. Then came the time for gifts; each great family gave something. Thank you! Thank you all!

Then, at a shout and a signal from the marabout. all the strong young men of Horodugu rose and cast off their robes. Stripped to the waist, they fell upon the cattle. Before being given the word, they overpowered them, tied them up, pinned them down and cut their throats. Great glittering knives thrust, cut and chopped. All amidst blood. But blood – you do not know this, because you are not Malinke – blood is stupendous, loud, gaudy, intoxicating. From far, very far away, birds see it blazing, the dead hear it, and it makes wild beasts drunk. Blood that flows is a life, a double escaping, and its sigh that we cannot hear fills the universe and wakes the dead.

Four head of cattle yield so much blood! The course of events could no longer be held back. The dogs went mad and charged. Until then pious and attentive behind the children, they were the first to be seized. All the seated Malinke leapt to arms, and together, wielding sticks, successfully defended themselves against the fangs of the pack. Successfully, in spite of the dogs' daring, because the men were more numerous by far. Beaten back, defeated, dispersed, the curs fell to quarrelling among themselves. They tore at each other's ears, gouged out each other's eyes, amidst infernal barking.

The men's second victory was against the birds of prey. Roused and maddened by the blood, they filled the sky and blotted out daylight. With wild cries, eagles and hawks formed squadrons and attacked, beak and talons to the fore, and their daring nose-dives threw the ceremony into a panic. The Malinke counter-attacked and won. The defeated birds scattered, soared and vanished in the coppery depths of the sky.

Best bring the ceremony to an end; everyone was exhausted, and animals and things were almost uncontrollably excited.

Amidst a feverish uproar, the calabashes and basins of food were quickly redistributed and removed. But when it came time to divide up the red meat, the sharing was done with care, equity and refinement, in accordance with the customs that allotted such-and-such a portion or cut to such-and-such a village or family, and in a short time it was all over, the four beasts dealt with and removed. Then the men broke the circle, scattered and moved off. All that was left was viscera and entrails, for the children.

Without being called, the brats rushed to seize their share; like dwarfish rope-makers they tugged at the intestines, swung them about, wound them round themselves. Very soon, in the time it would take to shout and snap your teeth, the brats scattered and vanished, as when a stone is tossed among the sparrows scratching about on the threshing-floor.

After the children, the dogs had their turns. There was nothing left, just a few pats of dung from the emptied entrails, many flies, and blood on the sand. The curs stopped their civil war, wolfed down the ordure and gobbled up the dust, pausing only to snap at the fowls that had sneaked in uninvited between their paws.

As a result, the birds were deprived of their share; everything had been licked up and picked clean without them. They reminded the men, by uttering sinister cries at sunset, that it was a sacrilege to have left them out. This threat cast a shadow over the festivities. People went to consult Balla. By worshipping the fetishes, the fetish-priest warded off the evil spells cast by the displeased birds.

Reassured, the men stopped worrying and devoted themselves to making merry. Right after last prayer the drumming began in the Dumbuya courtyard. It lasted all night long.

Because of the young girls' quivering breasts, pulsating buttocks and white teeth, let us skirt round the dancing: *yagba, balafon, ngume*. Let us sit down, however, and watch the hunters' *ngoni*. A bastard *ngoni*! Truly the suns of Independence are unsuited to great things; they have not only unmanned, but also unmagicked Africa. There was no startling wizardry to be seen, only a few little tricks that Fama had seen performed fifty times over by a European conjuror in the city.

A hunter thrust a needle into his left eye and drew it out of his anus. Another fired four fingers of hard-packed powder, with four bullets, in his right ear, and produced at his left ear a calabash full of water, containing the bullets. A third hunter (but remember, Balla could do this too) kept a gun floating in the air, between heaven and earth. Not one of them, however, summoned the fierce panther or solitary buffalo from the depths of the bush into the very dance-circle, to slaughter it there. Not one drop of blood! A hunters' dance, a *ngoni* without blood is admittedly disappointing. Disappointing, too, was the boom of the trade muskets. They frightened no one, not even the animals. Attracted and maddened by the scent of blood that still hung over the village that night, wild beasts had come down from the hills to howl beyond the compounds, and bulls bellowed ominously in their stalls. They could be heard even in the midst of the dancing, whenever the drummers paused to tighten and warm the heads of their drums.

These were highly successful funeral ceremonies. But how could you tell? For days afterwards Jamuru and Balla went over the countless favourable signs. An idiot, or a child only so high, would have noticed them. One certain sign was the throng of Malinke in attendance, more numerous than those the single party forces to dance when its president comes for a visit. Indeed, as always on such occasions, not all of those present were men. Balla, who had been thrust aside from the ceremony and seated just in front of the dogs and children, was well aware of it. At least eighteen of the people who passed by him smelled like spirits, shades, animals or devils.

Another undeniable sign was the universal turmoil. Only three times in his life had Balla witnessed such scuffling of beast and men for the blood shed at a ceremony; Jamuru had seen it only four times. It would seem therefore that since the suns of Samory, there had been only three or four funeral ceremonies as successful as that of the late cousin Lasina.

No need to go on about it, then. The sacrifice had been accepted, its purpose fulfilled. All the dead were happy, especially Fama's ancestors. Already the deceased Lasina had joined them. Now his double would never wander about behind the compounds, nor haunt men's dreams in search of the resting-place that would grant him peace.

A journey is something to study carefully; you consult the sorcerer, the marabout, you try and find out if the journey is auspicious or ill-omened. If auspicious, you toss the shades and spirits a sacrifice of two white kola-nuts, to thank them. If ill-omened, you give up the idea of the journey; if that is not possible (which may be the case) you wait a bit, and consult the marabout, the sorcerer; there are sacrifices to temper misfortune, even to ward it off. But the simple, clear, safe thing to do is to cancel an ill-omened journey. Who can say whether a sacrifice will be accepted?

Now tell me! Was Fama's journey to the capital city (for a month, he said), back to Salimata and his friends and acquaintances, to inform them that he intended to settle permanently in Togobala, and to put his affairs in order, now tell me truly, was that journey really necessary? Not at all! And the journey was extremely ill-omened. Only considerable sacrifices could temper fate, and to ward it off would require sacrifices extremely difficult to manage. Balla told him so, over and over again. Fama turned a deaf ear; he must go. There is a kind of foolhardiness that lures us to our doom.

What more did he need? In Togobala, within his reach, at his disposal were honour (as committee member and village chief), money (with Balla and Jamuru paying) and marriage (a fruitful young wife, Mariam). Why leave all that behind to set out on a dangerous journey?

No one can bypass his fate. Balla was amazed. After all, Fama, you may be the last of the Dumbuya and the master of Horodugu, but you were worth no more than Balla's grandson. Ignorant as you were of the things of old, as blind and deaf in the invisible world of shades and spirits as Balla was in our world, you should have heeded the old fetish-priest. To set out on an ill-fated journey could mean a pointless serious accident, or a dreadful illness, or death, or a plot against you...

Fama wanted to go, so go he would. And although he was certain that Salimata would give her a dog's welcome, he agreed to take Mariam along. Truly the undertaking of a man possessed!

They set out on foot from Togobala for the border town; there was a market there that day, and lorries stopped there on their way south. Two bearers and Mariam walked ahead, followed by Fama with his retinue. All the old men had come along: Baffi, Jamuru, Balla. The latter stopped after the last compound of the village.

'Master and son, I will leave you here. Uh! Uh! No one can fathom this world of the suns of Independence. A day is already long, it contains many things; what of a month then? And I am too old. Men's life under the suns of Independence is poised at the tip of their little finger, ready to take flight. If I die ... Uh! Uh!'

'But, Balla, you are still a long way from dying,' protested Fama.

'Let me speak; the sun is already high. Uh! Uh! Who has ever told you that he and death have agreed on a date? As I was saying, if I should die before your return, I will speak favourably of you to your ancestors underground, I will be very useful to you as a shade, and you in turn will not forget to toss me a piece of white kola-nut from time to time. Uh! Uh! ... In any case, never stay away long from your ancestors' graves; only in Togobala will a Dumbuya, a descendant of Suleyman, grow, prosper, flower and bear fruit.'

Let us add that after the travellers had left, the sun swiftly rose. But, and this was unheard-of in Horodugu in the middle of the dry season, clouds darkened the sky towards midday, and thunder rumbled and died away in the direction Fama had taken.

Truly an ill-omened journey!

PART THREE

10 *Things that cannot be talked about do not deserve a name*

They arrived in the capital city, Fama and his young wife Mariam, the widow of the late Lasina. The morning was damp and millet-coloured, like morning in a wood after a stormy night. They gathered up their belongings; all Mariam's calabashes had been trampled and crushed. A taxi carried them off (it was the first time she had rested her rear on the seat-cushions of a car) and deposited them, Mariam at a friend's house, and Fama at the west gate of the compound.

Salimata, delighted, ran to welcome Fama. That afternoon a palaver was called. Mariam came, and was introduced to Salimata:

'Here is your co-wife, consider her your little sister; the village people have sent her to help you in your magnificent work on behalf of your husband Fama.'

Salimata had joyfully greeted her co-wife, and explained with wit and feeling that a household with only one wife was like a stool with one leg, or a one-legged man; it can stand only by leaning on a stranger. But she was not to be believed, for this affectionate wisdom lasted exactly nine days.

Fama and his two wives lived in the little room, with its one *tara* or bamboo bed. The wife whose night it was slept next to the husband, the other curled up on a mat at the foot of the bed. But Salimata (as you will remember), in order to become fruitful, before going to bed would spend a long time praying, burning herbs, anointing herself, and dancing, dancing until she was breathless and beside herself. Spells, prayers and dancing were awkward now. Mariam was in the way; she was as insolent as a fly, and, it was said, as prolific as a mouse. Every morning upon waking Salimata would look at her co-wife's belly, and the belly seemed to be growing. Yes, it was growing! Salimata became jealous, then furious, and one morning she burst out with a volley of insults. The two wives flew at each other like two hens, each clutching the other's cloth. Mariam wanted to tear off Salimata's cloth, to let everyone see 'the shrivelled womb of a sterile woman', and Salimata wanted to strip Mariam, to show the world 'the great putrid thing of a whore'. They were pulled apart. Insults were exchanged all day and even at night, a night that belonged to Mariam. After prayers, they put out the lights and went to bed. Unfortunately, however, the *tara* creaked. Have you ever slept on a *tara*? It creaks and crackles as if you were rolling about in a heap of dry leaves in the middle of the harmattan season.

In the dark, therefore, once Mariam and Fama were in bed together, the *tara* creaked. Salimata howled:

'That creaking drives me mad!'

She danced about with rage, then flung herself on the bed. There was a struggle in the dark, like a fight between mudfish. The lamp was lit once more. Salimata ran outside and rushed back in brandishing a large knife, howling.

'Mad! mad! the creaking drives me mad!'

Mariam took refuge behind the bed. Fama and some neighbours managed to control the possessed woman. Both women had to spend the rest of the night on the floor, each on a mat. They did the same the following nights, for Salimata would not, could not sleep on the bed, even after her ritual. Fama made her tense and fearful, and above all the *tara* creaked; the creaking tore at her ears, stung her eyes, goaded her spirit. And when the night was Mariam's, there was always the same creaking, that sent her howling to fetch the knife, that made her want to kill.

Fama could have bedded Mariam during the day, while Salimata was at the market. He did not; custom forbade it. And Fama, who had always been so impetuous, in the matter of the enmity between his wives became a passive spectator. He claimed that the situation was like a young bull with neither horns nor tail; he didn't know how to handle it, how to take control. But what was happening between Mariam and Salimata had been foreseeable; don't gather birds together if you fear the sound of wings. Fama fully deserved his worries; they were like the flies that swarm about a man who insists on keeping a flock of toads.

Yet all things considered, his household was like a jar that is leaning over, but has not yet spilt its contents. There was hope. Where have you ever seen a tangle of string without an end to unravel it by? Nowhere. But you have to search for it, patiently, persistently. If you call your goats every evening, 'Come home! home! home!', they'll come home in the end. Fama didn't even want to call out 'Home! home!' He thought it would all come right in the end.

'Even mason-wasp and toad will come to terms if they're shut up in one room, so why not Mariam and Salimata?' he would say.

Best not worry about it, but spend as much time as possible away from home during the day, heed no one, take no notice of the quarrels and shouting. Indeed, the situation in the Ebony Coast gave Fama ample opportunity to follow this prudent rule.

The country seemed on the brink of insurrection. Night and day, Fama hurried from one palaver to another. The most unlikely and contradictory rumours were whispered from ear to ear. There was talk of plots, of strikes, of political assassination. Fama exulted. He visited his former political cronies, his associates during the period of anti-colonialism. They no longer concealed their anxiety; they were all afraid. Fama enjoyed hearing them say that anything could happen to the country, at any moment: arson, civil disorder, famine and death. In truth, Fama hoped that all these things would happen at once. And when he thought about it, it seemed inevitable that these calamities should occur, to sweep away the unlawful rule of sons of slaves.

Yes, it all had to collapse, if only because the republics of the suns of Independence had neglected to provide themselves with institutions such as fetishes or sorcerers, to ward off danger.

Throughout Africa, before the suns of Independence, a village could ward off misfortune by sacrifices. People sought to foretell, to unveil the future. It is not true that the future remains hidden, like a wild beast crouched in a thicket. Nothing happens without being announced: the rain warns the earth by wind, clouds and lightning that it is about to strike; as death does by dreams the man whose end is near.

The Malinke of Horodugu knew this well; they practised divination, and not only by the methods God prescribes. As Muslims at heart and at prayer, they should have outlawed the *koma* fetish. But the fetish saw further into the future than did the Koran; so they transgressed God's law, and every dry season the *koma* danced at the village meeting-place, to reveal the future and prescribe the appropriate sacrifices. And what Malinke village did not have its own oracles? Togobala, capital of all Horodugu, had two: a hyena and a python.

The oldest hyena in all the hills of Horodugu – respectfully called 'the Old One' – rarely howled at night in Togobala. All the village, women, men and children, could recognize its hoarse, toneless howl, and whenever the Old One was heard (it usually started before sunset) all fell silent, even the dogs. The old people of the village kept count on their fingers of the hoo-oom! The hyena came down from the hills, drew closer and closer, entered the village near the silk-cotton tree on the north side, passed compounds and huts and stopped at the foot of the baobab tree; there it howled, howled, scratched the ground, then fell silent. A goat or dog would be slaughtered for it. The Old One would snatch it and disappear into the silent night. The village once more began to hum with life. The elders of the village, Balla to the fore, would meet to interpret the message and decide on the appropriate sacrificial offerings.

And the serpent! As old as the Old One, as thick as the neck of a young bull, twenty paces long, it was called 'the Reverend of the creek'. 'Of the creek' because on cool mornings and evenings, it would lie sunning itself across the path that led to the creek. Passers-by would greet it and step over it. Women would lay clothes over it to dry, children would sit on it. It often roamed about behind the village, but never, night or day, come dry season or rainy, did it ever enter the village, except when it had a message to deliver, giving warning of misfortune to come and prescribing a major sacrifice. Then the serpent would leave the creek and rush like the wind towards Togobala, flattening the grass as it passed; through the village gate it would come, past the compounds and round and round the baobab tree; then it would rear up, breathless and foaming, from the baobab's hollow trunk. The news would travel through the village, and the great drum would be beaten.

Fama could still remember how the Reverend entered the village one Friday during the 1919 rainy season. It was flung a cock, that it disdained; then a ram, that it stunned, hugged, suffocated, crushed, coated with saliva and swallowed whole as far as the horns. For three days the python lay digesting the ram, three days during which many sacrifices were offered.

The results were fortunate, for three months later came the predicted calamity: the fearful plague known throughout Africa as the great sickness of the great wind. The disease devastated Horodugu, killing men and beasts and destroying several villages. In Togobala there were deaths and burials; but the village survived, thanks to the soothsayers, thanks to the python, thanks to the sacrifices offered, as God in his mercy had willed it.

Where were the *koma*, the hyena, the serpent, the soothsayers of the Ebony Republic? They had none. It was well known that the rulers of the suns of Independence often consulted marabouts and sorcerers; but for whose sake, and why? Fama knew the answer: it was never for the community's sake, never for the country; they always consulted sorcerers on their own behalf, to strengthen their rule, increase their power, cast evil spells upon their enemies. The calamities being foretold would surely occur; one of these nights they would be set in motion, and there would be nothing to soften or turn aside the blows of fate, as only well-judged sacrifices can.

At first, events seemed to prove Fama right. Anti-government slogans appeared on the walls of the capital. Strikes were being planned. One night a bomb exploded, and there were fires in nearby powder-factories. With or without sacrifices, with or without a hyena, the régime undertook to ward off the danger.

The president and the single party launched a wave of repression. Two ministers, two deputies and three councillors were publicly apprehended, taken to the airport, thrust on to aeroplanes and expelled. A special cabinet meeting was called; it lasted all afternoon, and ended in a great feast at the close of which four ministers were arrested on the steps of the presidential palace, handcuffed and taken to gaol.

All these were danger signals Fama should have heeded; he should have pulled hands and feet out of politics, and attended to his wives' quarrels. Politics has no eyes, no ears, no heart; in politics, true and false wear the same cloth, just and unjust go hand in hand, good and evil are bought and sold at the same price. Yet Fama continued to attend one palaver after the other, and to pay nightly calls on such-and-such a deputy, minister or adviser.

One day, one of Fama's former associates disappeared; another day two, then three. No doubt they had been arrested at night. Fama caught the first scent of smoke from the fire that threatened him; there was still time to flee. But he boasted:

'A Dumbuya, a real one, never turns his back on danger.'

He could not even see that those who were openly arrested or who disappeared, did not dance to the same drums as he did. They had all grown rich with Independence; they drove cars, spent banknotes as if they were dead leaves lying on the ground, often had four or five wives as peaceful as ewes and as prolific as mice. Fama persisted, shouting in palavers that he would not rest until his former friends had been set free. If the coucal has been caught in a snare, why should the bush-fowl roll about in despair, and declare it won't survive the night? If we take on too much of other people's troubles, misfortunes not meant for us may strike us down. Fama had refused to hear the thunder, his would be the storm and the lightning.

One night, as he was leaving a minister's villa with his friend Bakary, they were both assaulted, knocked down, man-handled and dragged to the president's palace, where they were thrust into the cellars. There Fama found all those he had been looking for. Like them, he had been arrested. It was in the cellars of the palace that he was first subjected to interrogation.

How many nights did he spend there? He did not know. In the cellar the lights were always on, and you could never tell when morning came or night began; you were tortured there, you breathed putrid air; you belly groaned with hunger; from time to time death rang out there, as did the drunken laughter of the gaolers draining bottles of alcohol. Thanks to the shades of the ancestors, and by the will of the Almighty, Fama survived.

One night he was dragged from the cellars, along with some of his fellow-prisoners; they were pushed into lorries, and at dawn they reached the gates of the camp where they were to be interned.

What was the name of this camp? It had no name, since the gaolers themselves did not know it. And that was as it should be. Things that cannot be talked about do not deserve a name, and the truth about this camp could never be told.

First of all, you lost all sense of time there. One morning you might figure out that you had been living there for years; that same evening, it would seem as if you'd only been there for a few weeks. That was because you arrived there half-dead, your mind full of nightmares, your eyes shut, your ears deaf. And you spent days there that were longer than months, and seasons shorter than weeks. The sun would suddenly shine in the middle of the night, and the moon appear at midday. At night you lay awake, and all day you staggered about, drunk with sleep.

Furthermore, Fama never found out in what part of the Ebony Republic the camp was located. He thought at first that it must be in the savanna region, in the remote wilderness of the Hugon Hills, because there were hills that hid from view both sunrise and sunset. But it wasn't in the savanna region: the seasons were those of the forest zone, the dry season short, with insignificant bush-fires that would light up the horizon for two or three nights. The rainy season was that of the forest, heavy and endlessly long; wind, storms and thunder raged and howled night and day, and the universe was in perpetual turmoil. But when he noticed that the flora and fauna were in some ways like those of the coast, Fama decided that the camp must have been built on an island or peninsula in the middle of the lagoons. For tsetse flies and mosquitoes were a constant torment; the damp lagoon air penetrated where their stings had pierced the skin, and the prisoners swelled up as if they all had double elephantiasis and triple beriberi. In the stagnant water about them swam and croaked large bright-coloured toads, and giant crocodiles would sometimes surface from among the water-lilies to fling themselves suicidally at the fence, unless the guards shot them first. In the evenings, Fama would hesitate. They weren't in the lagoons, because you could hear savanna bird-calls, the bark of monkeys, the roar of lions and the silence that follows and respects that roar in the deep of the night.

The camp was night and death, death and night. Everything there happened at night: supply deliveries, departures, arrivals, burials.

One night Fama was summoned and put in a lorry along with a few other detainees; at dawn they stopped in front of a barracks at the edge of a town. There you could hear some life, and hear morning come. They got out, and Fama was led to a cell where two other prisoners lay. They informed him that he had just arrived at Mayako Barracks, where preliminary investigations into the case were being conducted, and where the trial would be held. The examining magistrates were already there, and had started work. Fama's hearing would take place the following morning, at the latest.

Praise be to God! So Fama had escaped for good from the camp without a name: he was now a defendant with a record, who would be tried; he was no longer detained under the law governing detention on suspicion. Those who have been tried and sentenced know what they're in for, and with a bit of luck they may even be released; but those detained on suspicion are almost never set free. Only the president can release them, and a president of the suns of Independence never has the time.

Guards did in fact turn up the next morning: the examining magistrate had summoned Fama. So it was true!

The judges' villa was on the east side of the barracks; Fama and the guards passed row upon row of huts, skirted round a villa, crossed a parade-ground and a garden.

To his surprise, Fama suddenly felt pleased. Indeed there was cause for pleasure. The morning was as sweet as yam. The sun must have been bewitched by the clouds, for a single downy wisp of cloud had tamed it. The wind blew gently as if wafted from the banks of the nearby lakes, that you could see from the barracks. And the air was alive with the song and flutter of birds; quarrelling, they flew from coconut palms to coffee plantations, and descended in flocks on the gardens: egrets, sandpipers, curlews, lapwings. Fama and his guards had arrived.

The law was holed up in a large villa surrounded by gardens: judges, clerks of court and typists worked there, guarded by tirailleurs. Even the stairs were strewn with plates, coffee-cups, towels and shoes, and from the office (formerly the villa's sitting-room) you caught sight of other rooms with unmade beds and laundry hung up to dry, trousers, shirts and underwear slung in heaps over ropes, a tangled criss-cross web of ropes.

Fama was made to sit between two guards, a pace away from the examining magistrate's desk. The latter, casually dressed, freshly showered and shaved (he smelled of toilet soap and after-shave) was biting his nails. He had typical Fula features, narrow forehead, straight nose, thin lips, and was thumbing through the file with a nonchalant air, as if Fama did not exist. Was it pretence or conceit? Pretence, for he quickly shut the file, looked up, and as if to make up for lost time began to fire questions at Fama in a firm tone of voice, ending each question with 'Come on, let's have it!'

Fama answered. Yes, he was Fama Dumbuya, born about 1905 in Togobala (Horodugu).

'Your relations with Naku? What were you to Naku? Come on, let's have it!'

Fama had known Naku, the former minister said to have organized the plot. He was a Malinke, like Fama; he had a degree from Paris, and like all the young Malinke back from France he was rude enough to sniff like a ram at his mother's buttocks, and as arrogant as the penis of a circumcised donkey. Yes, Fama had known him. But how? Although he'd never managed to shake hands with him, Fama had twice ventured to call on Naku, in the hope of receiving at least the price of two kola-nuts, his right as a legitimate Dumbuya. The first time, at the ministry, after he'd been asked his name, first name, profession and address, a good-for-nothing of a messenger had informed him that the minister dealt with personal matters at his residence. One evening Fama had walked over there. In the bungalow, young Minister Naku was tickling a woman; you could hear them laughing from out in the garden, then the woman.... The magistrate interrupted Fama, and pointed out the torture chamber where they would be able to make him talk. No one was interested in how Naku handled his women; Fama was to make a statement about the dream and sacrifice, the dream about which Bakary had conveyed a message. Bakary had already talked; Fama was to confirm his story. 'Come on, let's have it!'

All eyes were on Fama, who could see the garden over the magistrate's shoulder, through the clothing hanging in the other room. The garden was beginning to come alive; the sun up there must have broken free from the spell cast upon it. There was a light breeze, mingling the palm fronds and ruffling the leaves and flowers of some bushes, the names of which Fama did not know.

Yes! It was true! Fama had had a dream, had been dazzled one night by one of those dreams that stay in your eyes for the rest of your life, as unforgettable as your circumcision day; the dream had concerned Naku. Yes, he had told Bakary about it. Ah! that was a dream that reeked of death, of fear!

First there was an atmosphere, a harmattan afternoon, with bush-fires. There were reptiles. Snakes or crocodiles? Fama could not tell; but they all had scales, and were wriggling up a tall anthill covered with greenish moss. Inside the anthill was the capital of the Ebony Coast. Looking down from the peak of the anthill into the pit within, that was like a grave emptied by hyenas, you could see the whole teeming city, swept by flames. Oddly, new-built walls stood here and there among the streets of ruined houses. How had they survived the fire? In the distance, smoke rose from two houses as if from two jars of incense at the feet of the dead. But where were the dead? As if echoing Fama's question, a baboon leapt out of the fire; it had claws of flame, flickering flame, and began to chase naked muscular men, maddened by terror, who fled before it; when it caught one it mounted him and took its pleasure as a dog does with a bitch, then leapt down sated, pursued another man (leaving in its wake a trail of fire), caught and mounted him. Praise be to God! The filthy ape spared Fama; but from the distant smoke in which it disappeared emerged a woman all veiled in white, except for her hands and feet which were black, the lustrous black of a crow's quill-feathers. Fama fled in terror, but the woman soon caught up with him.

'Come!' she said to Fama, 'let us talk. I, do you harm! Do not think that I am like that one,' she continued, meaning the baboon, and pointing with contempt to the place where the monster had vanished. 'I want to tell you something that concerns Naku,' she added.

Still terrified, Fama objected that he never saw Naku; besides,

'Why me, woman? Why tell me, when there are so many acquaintances of Naku's in the city, and besides...'

The woman interrupted Fama.

'To pass by one door, then a second, then a third, and stop at the fourth, means you are looking not for a particular house, but for a particular man.' She continued: 'Tell Naku to sacrifice an ox, and...'

She indicated many more offerings, but in such a low murmur that Fama could not hear; then she vanished. Fama looked for her in vain; she had completely disappeared. He kept searching, and came upon a man as naked as baobab trunk and tapered like a spindle, kneeling on the ground and touching the sand with his lips; suddenly inspired, Fama exclaimed:

'Ah! now I understand! A plot will cause Naku's downfall and devastate the city, but if Naku offers up the sacrifice, he will survive, and later on the conspirators will be unmasked and disgraced.'

At these words the veiled woman reappeared, radiant with joy.

'Yes, you have understood it all,' she said,' but remember that misfortune, whomever it may strike, is never a stranger to us, never remote, on the contrary... on the contrary... on the contrary...'

Fama woke petrified, the words 'on the contrary' still ringing in his ears.

'Could I possibly keep such an ill-omened dream to myself?' asked Fama. The magistrate, shaking his head, agreed that he could not. Well then, since he, Fama, did not want to go back to Naku's alone, he had told Bakary, who objected:

'Yes, it's our duty to tell him, but I know it's no use. These young men back from beyond the seas don't think like Africans any more.'

There was a moment's silence. Was it because Fama was the first to be examined that day, or because he was the first to admit taking part in the plot? All of them: clerks, policemen, typists, were listening intently.

The sun had spread throughout the garden, and from time to time insects seemed to cross his field of vision, blazing a bright trail in the air then fading in a halo of light. The heat was everywhere; armpits, groin and neck began to prickle all over. You had trouble breathing, you could hear your breath, and feel your sides, belly and nostrils palpitating; you saw ears strain to hear, eyes widen with effort, and you felt diminished, and above all powerless against everything that surrounded you. Fama's lips were dry (he had talked too much), thirst burned his tongue and irritated his throat. The magistrate broke the silence. Did Fama have anything more to say? No. They threatened him. No, nothing more. The typist produced a few clicks, then a clatter from his machine. Fama once more recounted his dream; the magistrate translated it into French, repeating phrases and stumbling over words, while biting the nails of his right hand.

He charged Fama with having taken part in a plot to assassinate the president and overthrow the Republic of the Ebony Coast. When Fama got up to leave, the magistrate asked him why, when he woke, he hadn't rushed to tell his dream to a prominent personality of the regime, the president, or the secretary-general of the single party. Fama did not answer.

'A pity! a pity!' exclaimed the magistrate. The dream would have been interpreted, and it would have been useful; many subsequent misfortunes would have been avoided. 'You may not have heard,' he added, 'but Minister Naku hanged himself in his cell, after admitting everything.'

For weeks, Fama waited to be told when the trial would be held. He could already see himself being acquitted, purely and simply acquitted. What had he done wrong? He had had a dream, and he could swear on the Koran that that was all; he had taken part in nothing else. On the day of the trial, he would begin by saying:

'Pay heed to this well-known proverb: the slave belongs to his master: but the slave alone is master of his dreams.'

Fama's dreams belonged to him, Fama. He could do as he wished with them. Indeed, who had ever told him that he was to recount his dreams to the rulers of the suns of Independence? And how could Fama, the last of the Dumbuya, be expected to sink so low as to go to the secretary-general of the party and say:

'Look here, secretary! Last night...'

The very thought of it made Fama angry. He didn't like the secretary-general. Hell and damnation! A curse on the suns of Independence! But be careful, Fama! On the day of the trial, control yourself, state things calmly; you might say, for instance, that you didn't know you were meant to tell the secretary about ill-omened dreams, or you might claim you had asked Minister Naku to inform him. In any case, Naku won't contradict you; he's dead and buried.

Thus for days and nights Fama muttered to himself what was to be his defence; he was still muttering, when one morning he was summoned before the examining magistrate.

When he arrived there between two guards, fifty-odd detainees were already waiting. The magistrate called the roll; then another file was laid before him, ceremoniously he opened it and carefully read out, with scrupulous attention to punctuation, an endless statement full of dialogue and subordinate clauses. Fama and many others could make nothing of it. A Malinke guard was instructed to translate what the magistrate was reading. This extempore interpreter must have been a Malinke from beyond the Bagbe river. He had a military style of speech, with short sentences.

'You are all jackals. You can't speak French and you tried to kill the president. That's what the judge said. He said the trial's over. So there. He know's you're all complainers, especially you Malinke, so he wants to make things perfectly clear. He wants to explain why the accused were not summoned for the trial. He considered there was no need. Each of the accused, in a statement freely made, had fully acknowledged that he was guilty. A good lawyer defended each case, and in each case sentence was passed by the president himself. And if anyone here wants to cast doubt on the president's sense of justice, just let him raise his hand. I'll knock it down myself. So there. All of you here are no-good Malinke, bastards; where I come from, no real Malinke would ever take part in a plot. Now open your rabbit ears and shut your hyena's-arse mouths. The judge is going to read out the sentences you richly deserve. So there.'

The judge read out the list of sentences. Fama had been given twenty years' solitary confinement with hard labour.

The prisoners were then led back to their cells, and the very next day Fama began his life as a convict.

Twenty years in prison, for Fama, was the equivalent of a life sentence. Now Fama had what he'd asked for. He would die in Mayako and be buried in Mayako, he would never see Horodugu again, nor Salimata. It was as clear as the palm of a frog. He'd been warned. The people of Independence know neither truth nor honour; they are capable of anything, even swallowing a bee. He'd been told: where thorns pierce the guinea-fowl's eggs, there the sheep must not go. He had gone ahead, he had wanted to overthrow the suns of Independence, and he had been defeated. Now he was like the hyena that fell down a well; there was nothing for it but to await God's will; to await death.

Sometimes he thought about the force that had lured him on, provoking the senseless foolhardiness that had landed him in this hole. He, Fama, had not heeded the great sorcerer Balla's prophetic words, when he left Togobala. Incredible as that now seemed to him, it was true. Why had Fama been so stubborn? Because he was pursuing his fate. Balla's words went unheeded, because they bounced off the eardrums of a man lured on by his fate, the fate ordained for the last of the Dumbuya.

'Fama, there's no doubt about it now, you are the last of the Dumbuya. That is as a clear as a full moon in a harmattan sky. You are the last drop of the great river that dies out and dries up in the desert. That was said and written centuries before your time. Accept your fate. You will die in Mayako. The Dumbuya will end in Mayako, not in Togobala.'

Thus he murmured to himself. Then he would resolutely think about something else.

Fama was not made to perform hard labour, but his health was deteriorating. Guinea-worm swelled in his armpits and knees. He was drying up; his eyes sank into sockets deeper than graves, his fleshless ears stood out like those of a hare on the alert, his lips grew thin and taut, his hair scanty.

11 *The wild birds were the first to understand the significance of what had happened*

In spite of his state of health, he woke every morning before cock's crow in order to say his morning prayer, the soothing prayer that prepares you to face the shades of your ancestors and the judgement of God. In truth, he was glad that his life was coming to an end. There were very few things he was sorry about; one of them was Salimata. Fama had always said to himself that a few moments before his death, he would call Salimata and ask her to forgive him the years of unhappiness he had caused her to live. Now he would not be able to do so. But God acknowledged good intentions. God had ordained that a woman's way to heaven was earned by being dutiful towards her husband. Then God could prepare Salimata's resting-place in his eternal heaven. She had done her duty, more than her duty. She had suffered for others' sake and Fama's, without receiving her reward from God. Fama was sorry, too, that his remains would not be laid to rest in the earth of Horodugu. He now saw that they had lied, all the marabouts, all the sorcerers and sooth-sayers who had constantly predicted that he was destined to arrive in Togobala one morning, escorted by a wondrous retinue, and to die in Horodugu, to be buried in the cemetery where his ancestors lay. None of that was true; unless . . . God's power is without limit.

These days spent pondering the melancholy thought of death, filled Fama's nights with dreadful dreams.

One morning, a few moments before he awoke, a dream flashed before his eyes. And what a dream! A voice called out to him:

'Look at yourself! Look at yourself! You are alive and strong. You are great. Admire yourself!'

Astride a white charger, Fama was flying or rather floating, his white robe fluttering in the wind, his stirrups and spurs of gold, escorted by a throng of gold-bedecked courtiers. A true Dumbuya! Authentic! The prince of all Horodugu, the only one, the great, the greatest of all. Beneath him something was fleeing, a lack, a desire, something that had slipped through his fingers. Was it a horse? A woman? Fama leaned over, but he couldn't make anything out, the something was as swift as the wind, and glowed like the trail of a distant bush-fire. Fama galloped after it, until he was near exhaustion; it fled faster and faster, it was on the point of disappearing, and you felt that if it disappeared, the world would be left bereft in empty-hearted misery. Yet Fama exulted, saying to himself:

'The thing won't escape, there's someone standing in its path, solid as rock, who won't let it go.'

Intoxicated with joy, Fama burst out laughing, laughing like mad; he laughed so loudly that he woke up, and once awake kept on laughing until ...

It was morning, the sun was high and filled the cell with its blaze. The air seemed to be crackling, deafening after deep sleep and loud laughter. The hour of first prayer was past; it would be absurd to bow down with the sun so far gone. Bursts of laughter, voices, whistling and footsteps could be heard on the other side of the door. Intrigued, Fama pricked up his ears: the whole barracks was humming, rustling with the sound a storm makes in a forest. He was about to listen more closely, when the door opened. Guards presented Fama with a new pair of baggy trousers, and a robe, fez and slippers, also new. Fama was to put them on immediately, and come with them. While dressing he noticed that on the parade-ground in the middle of the barracks, workmen and soldiers were busy giving the final hammer-strokes to the grandstand they had erected during the night, and arranging chairs and benches in rows. There was a jumble of parked cars behind the barracks.

As Fama went off with the guards, they told him that since early morning cars had been arriving from all the provinces of the republic. All the ministers, secretary-generals, deputies, economic advisers and generals were already there. But they had no time to tell him more; they had arrived at the parade-ground. The guards seated Fama on a bench, among other detainees. Behind the stand, praise-singers, drummers, xylophones and horns formed a dense many-coloured throng. Officials were arriving, choosing a place and sitting down.

Suddenly the metallic tones of the women praise-singers rang out, followed by the cries of the men; and all the musical instruments resounded together. Then the president, yes! the president of the Ebony Republic himself made his appearance, followed by all the prominent figures of the régime. The din of shouting and drumming continued until he had majestically established himself at the place of honour in the grandstand. Then the secretary-general made a gesture, and all was still. He announced that the president was about to make an important speech. The head of state rose. Pandemonium broke out again, but a second gesture from the secretary-general restored silence. The president strode forward, and his gaze swept the captivated crowd. A guard at once adjusted the microphone, into which the head of state blew loudly to clear his throat. Applause, drumming and the praise-singers' shouting started up again. For the third time, the secretary-general had to intervene to obtain silence. This time, the speech began; the president spoke. At first he spoke softly, quietly, in the low, persuasive tone of voice of which he alone held the secret.

He talked and talked, about the brotherhood that binds all black men together, about humanism in Africa and the good-heartedness of Africans. He explained what it was that made our country peaceful and hospitable: willingness to forget past offences, love of one's neighbour, love of our country. Fama could not believe his ears. From time to time he would thrust his little finger into his ears, to clear them; he kept wondering if he were not still dreaming. But amazingly, it was all being said. It was true, it wasn't a dream; it was real. The president was asking the detainees to forget the past, to forgive him, to think only of the future, 'the glorious future we all hope for'. All the prisoners were to be set free.

'Every single one. At once. All their possessions would be restored to them.'

As the president often paused to emphasize important words or phrases, his speech was interrupted by sudden sharp bursts of din.

Why had he, the President, taken this decision? For very important reasons. He, the president, was the mother of the republic, and all its citizens were his children. A mother is sometimes compelled to be strict with her children. A mother will deal very harshly with her children, if they spill on the ground the dish of rice she has prepared for her lover. And his, the president's lover was the country's economic development; the plot was endangering this future, spilling it on the ground. One reason he had decided to free them, with full knowledge of the case, was that wickedness, anger, injustice, impatience, villainy and evil are temporary states, like illness, whereas goodness, gentleness, justice and forbearance are like health; they can be permanent. The political unrest and constant strife in the country had undermined the president's international prestige.

'Investors were turning away, newspapers discussed my imminent downfall, the presidents of neighbouring states slighted me.'

Our ancestors' sayings were still true; the most beautiful harmony is not sounded by drums, xylophones or trumpets; it is harmony between men.

'A single foot cannot tread out a path; and a single finger cannot lift the smallest pebble.'

He, the President, could not build the country alone. It was a task for everyone. However great the country where disharmony reigns, it can be destroyed in a day. The detainees were all being freed, so that the country would be at peace. The drumming and applause flared up again. Each detainee could ask for whatever he wanted: the party and the government would grant it. Ex-prisoners who were in poor health would receive treatment; if necessary, they would be sent to the great hospitals and health resorts of France or America.

'Long live the Ebony Republic! Long live our heartfelt reconciliation!'

Applause, drumming and shouting hailed the end of the speech, and went on and on. The secretary-general and the president had all the trouble in the world restoring silence; the musicians and dancers had thought the festivities were to begin. When silence fell, the president concluded with these words:

'This enthusiastic response will show our brothers, better than long speeches, how happy the people are that they are now free to return to their homes.'

The president then had all the former prisoners introduced to him. He embraced them one after the other, and presented each one with a thick wad of banknotes. Of course, each embrace was greeted with shouts, applause and a burst of drumming. Then the programme of the Reconciliation Day festivities was announced:

'The main celebrations will take place in the capital city. The released prisoners will tour the city in open cars. The liars who said they were all dead will be contradicted by the facts. There will be fireworks at nine o'clock, followed by a state dinner. The festivities will conclude with balls and dancing until dawn.'

The president had finished.

Relatives and friends rushed up to the detainees and bore them away. Everyone got into cars. They were to set out for the capital city straight away. The cars started one after the other.

Fama was travelling with his friend Bakary, who kept hugging him.

'Have no regrets,' he said, 'you'll have a good time now.' A hug. 'You have money, and you'll soon have more.' A hug. 'It's true you don't look too good, but the president said you'd be able to go wherever you liked to get back into shape. If I were you, I'd go to Vichy. Yes, Vichy, that's where all the millionaires go.' Another hug. 'And you can have whatever position you want. If I were you, I'd ask to be made director of a co-operative.' A hug. 'You see that misfortune is sometimes just good fortune well wrapped up; when the wrapping wears away, good fortune tumbles out. We who were released before you had no such luck. When it comes right down to it, Fama, you've been lucky. That prison was your good luck.'

Bakary tried to hug him, but Fama motioned him away with his fist. Bakary didn't insist; perhaps he realized that Fama had not said a single word since they had caught sight of each other, and regretted his enthusiastic remarks. It was Bakary's turn to start his car and join the procession.

Bakary drove off in silence; once the car had left the barracks, he began to talk again, but this time more calmly. He could understand why Fama was silent. All the detainees' wives, except Fama's, had come to fetch their husbands. No need to worry much about women, though; if you have money, you can have women. Fama's wives had no self-respect; they knew no shame, not so much as would cover the palm of your hand. Now that Fama had money, he should get himself some other wives. There would be parents prepared to give him their daughters. If he, Bakary, were in Fama's shoes, he would choose a plump, hot little number; he'll introduce Fama to a few some time. Salimata and Mariam had really behaved very badly. And Bakary told what had happened in Fama's compound during his absence.

As soon as the women had heard of his arrest, they had rushed to find replacements.

Salimata went back to consult Abdullahi, the marabout she had stabbed with a knife still red with the blood of the sacrificial cock. Abdullahi no longer frightened her, no longer reeked of Chekura. And Mariam? Since she was just in from the bush, and therefore undiscriminating, she took what was ready to hand: the taxi-driver who had picked her up the day she arrived in the city. This taxi-driver's name was 'Little by little', but Bakary preferred to call him 'Butterfly', because his taxi, a Dauphine, had the name 'Butterfly Independence Jazz' inscribed in four colours across the rear window, and because he himself dressed in butterfly finery: green scarf, tricolour straw hat (the three national colours), white rimmed sunglasses, casually unbuttoned red shirt, yellow trousers, scuffed sandals. He was a slim youth, tall, as black as a deaf-mute, but as rude as the rear end of a bitch big with pups. Night and day he would flit by the gate, race his motor and sound his horn. Mariam would come out. Butterfly took her for drives, and she could never have enough of riding in a car.

It was a disgrace! As deep a disgrace as that which drove the monitor lizard to hide in the river. The whole neighbourhood was gossiping. In the end, Bakary couldn't stand it any more. One day he had said to himself:

'Is Fama my friend, or isn't he? He's still my friend. It's true we parted company just before Independence; but who didn't quarrel then? He's a true prince, and a prince is always difficult to live with. In spite of everything, he's still a friend of mine. You can't share your friend's death, but if he's humiliated, heaped with shame, you share his disgrace.'

So Bakary had seized Butterfly by the scruff of the neck, one morning on a street-corner, and told him straight out:

'Everyone knows you're leading Mariam astray. Aren't you ashamed, Butterfly, to be playing around with an older man's wife? Watch out, Butterfly, Mariam's husband's name is Dumbuya, and he's a real prince; he'll come back. He's not like the men of Independence, and he'll never forgive you for having stuck your penknife into his dagger's sheath. Even if you flee, misfortune will pursue you, because Mariam has a spell on her. She hasn't told you, because her wits don't reach any further than the tip of her breasts. Balla, the greatest sorcerer of Horodugu, put a spell on her, and if you keep going with her, Butterfly, you can be certain that one day, sooner or later, your penis will disappear; it'll be swallowed up in your belly like a rifle stuck in quicksand.'

Butterfly hadn't turned a hair: when Bakary released him, he walked away, and back in his car he had shrugged his shoulders.

Fama remained silent and thoughtful. The parade was advancing through a constant uproar, that irritated him.

'Why don't you say anything?' asked Bakary.

Fama did not answer. Bakary once more began to talk. He knew that Fama was ill, that his health had been seriously affected, but all life was in God's hands. He reassured Fama: death would not come for him during the next few years. For he, Bakary, knew death; it had many faults, it lied and deceived, but it would never take a man like Fama, who had come into money for the first time in his life. Then, after a moment's silence, as if he regretted having mentioned death to a man who was ill, Bakary exclaimed:

'I was forgetting to tell you about Togobala, all the news from Togobala; and he told what had happened in Horodugu while Fama was in prison.'

A pedlar up from the south had announced Fama's arrest to the people of Togobala. It was as much of a shock to them as a death would have been! The sacred drum was sounded, the committee and the council of elders met for a palaver, beasts were slaughtered in sacrifice.

When the news was shouted in Balla's ear, he showed no surprise: he was expecting it. The old fetish-priest, usually as cautious as a lizard with its tail cut off, declared straight away:

'Fama will never again see Togobala.'

He could be wrong; his fetishes, shades and spirits were probably beginning to desert him, for death was drawing near to the old babbler.

One night the Old One, the hyena, the oracle of Togobala, came down from the hills and howled, standing in the village meeting-place under the baobab tree. They tossed it a goat, and interpreted its howls; their meaning was:

'One old and venerable thing will be defeated by another.'

That was in the middle of the rainy season. Yet for four days rain-clouds vanished from the sky. The fifth morning came before its time, but the sun did not rise: space was stretched taut as a drum, with a feeling of strangeness seeping in from the horizons. There was none of the usual morning bird-song, and no flight of vultures from the trees. Everything was quiet and still. All eyes turned towards Balla's front door; it was still shut tight. When they opened it, they found that sleep had betrayed the old fetish-priest; death had struck while he was asleep, and he was stiff and cold.

The drums had then sounded throughout Togobala, and the news echoed from rivers, forests and hills, until it reached other villages where other drums began to beat, to alert other villages still further away.

All Horodugu breathed a great 'Ah!' of surprise, and earth, beasts and things came back to life. The sun burst forth, but remained motionless until the hour of second prayer, when it was overcast by the shower of rain that always falls when the grave of a great man is dug in Horodugu, to soak the ground before it is broken.

As Balla was a heathen, he was buried without prayers, and on the west side of Togobala, rather than the east where Muslims are buried.

But there were splendid ceremonies for the seventh-day and for-tieth-day funeral rites (four head of cattle!). The hunters performed more magical wonders than ever before, and many spirits, animals and dead men attended the ceremony in human form, to pay a last homage to the deceased's wisdom and experience. Ah! it will be a long time before Horodugu sees Balla's like for knowledge! After a few moments' silence, Bakary deployed all his verve in an exag-gerated account of the old sorcerer's last exploits (or last tricks). He wanted to rouse Fama, to shake a word or at least a sigh from him! But they had arrived. Bakary had to stop talking. The city was throbbing with the National Reconciliation Day festivities. He glanced sideways at his still silent and pensive companion, and began to drive with the care required in the midst of the city's festive turmoil. The procession of cars had entered the main avenue of the city, lined on both sides with a frenzied and colourful crowd. Drums were beating, praise-singers singing, and men and women were dancing on the pavement, in the gutters and the public squares. When their car drew level with the road station from which lorries left for the north, Fama made a gesture. Bakary said they couldn't stop:

'You can't stop when you're in an official procession.'

Fama shouted 'Stop!' and accompanied the order with the peremptory commanding gestures of the last descendant of the Dumbuya. Bakary realized that he would have to comply straight away, without arguing. He pulled over to the side of the road, and braked.

Fama opened the car door, got out and walked away. Bakary put on the handbrake and ran after him, to try and persuade him. Fama was making a mistake. Where was he going? Now that he could have anything he wanted, why didn't he want to carry on with the celebrations, like the others? Was it because of the women that he was leaving? But you can always buy yourself women. Didn't he want any fresh young girls? Then Salimata was here. She was a respectable woman, who would come back to Fama if he wanted her. Salimata still loved Fama, and it was only in order to have a child that she had gone to the marabout; in fact, that was why Bakary hadn't threatened the marabout or molested him in any way. Fama continued to make his way through the crowd. The road station was at the far end of a square swarming with dancers. Fama skirted round a circle of xylophone players, slipped between two drummers, retraced his steps in order not to be crushed by some acrobats turning somersaults in the air, avoided the jugglers and the people beating out tunes on calabashes filled with water, and reached the road station.

Bakary was still following him; at one point he thought of clutching at the sleeve of Fama's robe, but in view of the predictable violent reaction he gave up the idea, and pressed Fama with ever more persuasive and honeyed words.

'Listen, Fama! You mustn't leave just when you can have money and a position, when you can become somebody and be useful to your friends and relations. What will you do in Togobala? The chiefdom is dead. Togobala is finished, it's a ruined village. You're not a leaf on a tree, that turns yellow and falls when the season changes. The suns have turned over with the colonial period and independence; let these new suns keep you warm! You're not a tiger-cat that chooses to die of hunger rather than eat the meat it's given, just because it's not the meat of its own killing. Be adaptable! Accept the world as it is! Or is it for Balla's funeral rites that you want to go up there? But funeral rites can always wait. Stay, Fama! The president is prepared to pay, in order to be forgiven the deaths he has on his conscience, and the tortures he made you all endure; he's prepared to pay so you won't talk about what you've seen. Take advantage of it! Let's both enjoy what your troubles have brought you. The money in your pocket is just one grain of corn, compared to the sackful you'll be given later.'

Fama strode proudly forward, as if Bakary's words weren't

addressed to him. When he came to a half-full lorry, the prince calmly climbed aboard.

The other passengers moved over to give Fama room to lie down, because he was visibly exhausted. The last Dumbuya took the place without thanking or even greeting them, because he believed they had made room for him to honour a prince.

Bakary could not bear to stay down on the ground; he leapt into the lorry and began upbraiding Fama.

'Fama, you don't know anything about life. You've lived like a vulture and you'll die like one. Do you think all men are subjects of Horodugu? You'll die in Togobala. Yes, you'll die in poverty, while here you can be of use to us: you can have something of your own, you can help your friends. When I heard you were going to be set free, and everything they were going to promise you, I was glad, and now ...'

The lorry-driver interrupted Bakary, and asked him to get out. They were leaving now.

As the lorry started and slowly moved off, Bakary had time to shout from the pavement:

'Fama, on your dying day you'll remember that you were a false friend. I was counting on you to support me for the rest of my life, and help me make some money too. Now you've ruined everything, you're no friend of mine.'

That was Bakary's farewell. Because of the National Reconciliation Day festivities, the lorry had to make a long detour before leaving the city. Fama didn't want to see the city again, its buildings, its streets, its people; he didn't want to breathe its air. He breathed a loud 'Ugh!' of disgust, closed his eyes and began to think.

Suddenly Fama burst out laughing. All the other passengers, startled, looked at the gaunt, emaciated old man, his eyes shut tight like a blind man's, laughing like mad. Now that Bakary was far away, Fama was laughing at his perplexed and disappointed friend, who must have stood on the platform watching the lorry leave. Fama was glad to have held him up to ridicule by remaining silent. Chat between panther and hyena honours the latter but lowers the former. As suddenly as he had started, Fama stopped laughing and began to think once more.

Why did he want to leave? Why was he overcome with revulsion at the very thought of staying, of living in the city again, as if at the thought of eating vomit? His eyes still shut, Fama listened for a time to the distant sounds of celebration, and the whispers of his fellow-passengers who must all be staring at him.

Fama wanted to leave because he knew that no one in the city wanted him, no one cared about him. Bakary didn't care about him; it was only because he needed someone to live off for a while, that his 'friend' had seemed happy to see him again. And Salimata didn't want him either. Yes! Salimata, the only person he would have liked to see again, didn't want him any more. What had kept Salimata by him these past few years, was not love, nor the sacred ties of marriage, nor the long memories they shared. What had held Salimata captive within their marriage, was that she couldn't stand to live with anyone else. Now, it seemed, for the first time in her life, Salimata was able to be with another man. Perhaps she loved him. Perhaps she was going to have a child. Perhaps she was happy. Fama hoped so. It was his duty not to trouble Salimata's happiness by appearing once more in the city, where his presence would have been a constant moral, reproach to her. She deserved a few days of happiness. Salimata, may you be happy, with no regrets, and sing every morning at your mortar that dance tune you like to sing when you are really happy:

> Hey! Hey! Hey! Hey!
> If falling down the well will bring good fortune,
> Hey! Hey! Hey! Hey!
> By all means let's fall down the well.

Mariam did not care about Fama either, and would not want to see him again. But Mariam wasn't worth a grain of regret, a drop of worry. Marrying her had been a mistake. The only thing about that marriage that gave Fama any satisfaction, was that it had helped Salimata to detach herself from him, had forced her to try and live with another man, thus laying the foundations of Salimata's future happiness.

Did that mean that Fama was going to Togobala in order to make a new life for himself? No, not at all! As paradoxical as it may seem, Fama was going to Horodugu in order to die as soon as possible. It had been predicted, centuries before the suns of Independence, that Fama was to die near the graves of his ancestors; perhaps it was that destiny that accounted for Fama's surviving the torture sessions in the cellars of the president's palace, and life in the camp without a name; and accounted for this astonishing liberation, that cast him once more out into the world when he thought he had taken leave of it forever.

At Mayako, praying long and often, he had resigned himself, he had come to accept his fate, and was ready to meet the shades of ancestors, ready for the judgement of God. Death had become his sole companion; they knew and loved each other. Fama already bore death within him, and life meant nothing to him but pain. At Mayako, everything was certain. But this startling liberation and sudden wealth was a kind of resurrection, casting Fama once more out into the world, and compelling him to make new plans, cherish new hopes, and start to love, hate, sorrow and struggle all over again. Fama had had enough of all that. A saying came to his mind, that Malinke sing when great misfortune strikes:

> Ho, sorrow! Ho, sorrow! Ho, sorrow!
> If you find a mouse on a cat-skin
> Ho, sorrow! Ho, sorrow! Ho, sorrow!
> Everyone knows that death is sorrow.

Fama opened his eyes. The lorry was leaving the city. Evening was near. Soon they reached the top of a hill overlooking the city.

The whole city seemed caught up in the National Reconciliation Day festivities. Everything was jumping, you could tell by the rooftops and the clumps of trees, that swayed and whirled; everything was soaring, you could tell by the way the streets, bridges and gardens floated and flowed together. Even a little train clinging to the cliffs above the lagoon, like a file of ants finding obstacles in its path, swung tirelessly round a thousand bends. Lower down and nearer, the only stretch of lagoon still lit by the sun was quivering to the beat of the singing and drumming. Fama wanted to break free of this giddiness, that drew everything into the frenzied orbit of the festivities. He sat up, and leaned out to try and make out a single recognizable roof, tree, street or bridge. It was over now, he was leaving; it was time to take a last look at the place where Salimata was. But it was too late; just then, the lorry started down the other side of the hill, the city disappeared and night began to fall. It was all over. Fama closed his eyes and dozed.

He woke early in the morning. During the night the lorry had reached the border, at the edge of the river, inside Horodugu. Fama was on the soil of Horodugu! Everything belonged to him here, even the river flowing at his feet, the river and the sacred crocodiles that inhabited it here. Bastard colonial era, bastard Independence!

If it had not been for the European conquest and the suns of Independence, there would have been celebrations, drumming, praise-singers to greet him upon waking; a retinue would have escorted him. But all that was over and done with, he didn't care about it any more. Let next dry season's crop of sorghum be plentiful or not, a dying man doesn't care.

Several other lorries that had arrived before Fama's were parked by the side of the road. To the left of the road, travellers with their wives and children were sleeping on mats around fires. To the right, the border guards' huts and the customs post could not be seen clearly in the mist. The road was blocked by a thick tangle of barbed wire at the entrance to the bridge. In the two tall watch-towers overlooking the scene, glinted the gun-barrels of the guards on sentry-duty. You sensed rather than saw, on the far side of the bridge, the other side's watch-towers amidst the foliage of the silk-cotton trees. A thin mist filled the valley. There was no wind.

It was the weaver-birds that started. They filled the clumps of silk-cotton and mango-trees with twittering and cheeping. The cocks began to crow. At first the dogs replied with their usual morning barking, but they soon set up a death-howl so sinister that it nearly tore the soul from your body.

That could well be a sign of an ill-omened day ahead. That was why the vultures and swallows perched on trees and rooftops took flight, soaring high in the sky to drag out the sun. They succeeded; the sun appearing at once. The dogs fell silent, their tails between their legs; the sacred crocodiles came out of the water, and after brief quarrels over precedence lay on the sandbanks and closed their eyes, the better to enjoy the first rays of the sun.

Fama felt revived and heartened by the good Horodugu morning air.

'Horodugu is the best place to live and die,' he murmured.

He regretted all the years spent among bastards in the capital city, then breathed deeply several times before turning to make his morning obeisance to God. But the calm lasted only a few moments. The dogs rushed back out and started up their death-howl again. The door of the customs post opened, a guard emerged, ran after the curs and reduced them to silence by pelting them with stones and hitting them with a stick. After this victory, he walked towards the barbed wire at the foot of the watch-tower.

All the travellers rushed to hear the latest news; those who were by the fires rose, and those who were in the lorries got out. Everyone crowded about the border guard who had just silenced the dogs. He was tall, elegant in his uniform, and above all (as Fama would find out later) very polite and friendly, like a man from before the colonial era, before Independence. His name was Vassoko. When Vassoko reached the barbed wire, he turned to face the crowd of travellers, and after a few smiles and pleasantries announced that he had received no telegram that night, and that the situation had not changed since yesterday. He was about to stop there, when he noticed some new faces; he apologized, and explained what he meant by 'since yesterday'. The border was shut until further notice, in both directions; all traffic was suspended for the moment. This measure had been in force for the past month. It was due to strained relations between the two countries. A shout of dismay greeted these explanations. Without losing his smile, the guard replied that the measure was the result of a political decision, and he could not even indicate when the border might be open once more. However, travellers who wished to camp beside the customs post might do so, sleeping round log fires as many people were already, provided they didn't make too much noise. Last night the chief of post had been awakened by the travellers' laughter. That was not to happen again.

The discontented travellers broke up and moved away, all except Fama. Clearly the prince of Horodugu could not be satisfied with the border guard's explanations. Vassoko greeted Fama with the same smile, and spoke. He, Vassoko, and the others were only carrying out orders, and their task was not an easy one. The laws, orders and decrees of the suns of Independence were as numerous as the hairs of a goat, as complicated as the genitals of a duck.

'Here at least is an intelligent guard, one you can talk to without losing your temper,' thought Fama.

So the last of the Dumbuya introduced himself to Vassoko, spoke of the geographical boundaries of Horodugu and the grandeur of its ruling dynasty, explained that he was ill and had to attend Balla's funeral rites. But the guard promptly replied that no one would allow Fama to pass; even if they were to let him through, the guards on the other side would not admit him to the Republic of Nikinai.

Vassoko asked to see Fama's papers. The prince didn't even have any identity card. Vassoko smiled briefly. No one could pass without papers. The last of the Dumbuya declared that he was an ex-political prisoner. The guard once more smiled briefly. Their instructions were not to let ex-political prisoners out of the country.

Fama felt anger well up in him, burning his armpits, his neck, his back. The sun was already high. The mist had vanished. The Dumbuya prince looked about for a stone, a stick, a gun, a bomb, something he could use to kill Vassoko, his superiors, Independence, the world. Luckily for all of us there was nothing to hand, and the guard may have perceived the danger, since he walked away and left Fama standing deep in thought in front of the barrier.

The sound of Vassoko's footsteps moved off and died away. Fama could make out the hum of travellers' voices near the lorries, and the murmur of a telephone conversation. Perhaps the guard had spoken to his superiors, perhaps the purpose of the telephone conversation was to have Fama taken to the dispensary of the nearest administrative subdivision, from which he would undoubtedly be evacuated to the capital city. Fama was in Horodugu, he must not let them take him away. The barbed-wire barrier was a few steps away. There was a door in it on the left side. Did a Dumbuya, a real one, father Dumbuya, mother Dumbuya, need permission from all the bastard sons of dogs and slaves to go to Togobala? Of course not. As coolly as you please, as if he were strolling out into his garden, Fama pulled open the door and found himself on the bridge. He set his cap straight, folded back the sleeves of his robe, and proudly, like a true panther totem, walked towards the other end of the bridge. After a few paces, fearing that all these children of the colonial era and of Independence might take his departure for flight, he stopped and shouted at the top of his voice, like one possessed:

'Look at Fama! Look at Salimata's husband! Look at me, you sons of bastards, sons of slaves! Watch me go!'

The travellers cried out in astonishment. The sentries on duty in the watch-towers called out a first warning:

'Halt!'

Vassoko rushed out of the customs post, and while running shouted to the sentries:

'Don't shoot! He's crazy! crazy!'

With his usual dignity Fama walked a few steps more, then stopped again and slowly enunciated these words:

'Look at Dumbuya, prince of Horodugu! Look at Salimata's lawful husband! Admire me, sons of dogs, sons of Independence!'

'Halt!'

'He's crazy. Don't shoot. I'll catch hold of him.'

Vassoko had quickly reached the barrier, passed through it and was running on the bridge. Fama was already at the other end, in front of the Nikinai Republic barrier, and was looking for a way through. But the strands of barbed wire were closely interwoven, and there was no gap through which you could so much as put your fist. In despair, Fama looked back. The guard was running towards him. Fama walked the length of the barrier. There was no way to climb over. He looked back once more: Vassoko was halfway across the bridge, he was going to catch up with Fama. But a Dumbuya doesn't let himself be captured like an exhausted hare. Fama walked over to the left side of the bridge. The parapet wasn't high, and beneath the bridge was the bank of the river. The big sacred crocodiles of Horodugu would never dare attack the last descendant of the Dumbuya. Vassoko was only a few steps away. Fama clambered on to the parapet and dropped on to a sandbank. He stood up; the water wasn't even knee deep. He was about to take a step forward when he saw a sacred crocodile rushing towards him like an arrow. On the banks of the river, they heard a cry. A shot rang out: a sentry had fired from one of the Nikinai Republic watch-towers. The wounded crocodile bellowed horribly, rending the earth and splitting the sky; in a flurry of blood and water it dashed under the bridge, where it continued to writhe and bellow.

As always in such circumstances in Horodugu, the wild animals were the first to realize the historical significance of the man's cry, the beast's bellow and the gunshot that had just shattered the morning peace. They showed it by behaving strangely. The birds: vultures, hawks, weavers, doves, uttering strange cries, took flight from the trees, but instead of soaring they swooped down upon the land animals and men. Startled by this unusual attack, the wild beasts charged towards the village compounds, the crocodiles rushed from the water and fled into the forest, while men and dogs, amid infernal shouting and barking, scattered and fled into the bush. The forests multiplied the echoes, and created winds to carry to the furthest villages and deepest graves the cry of the last Dumbuya. Throughout all Horodugu the echoes of the cry, the bellow and the gunshot created the same astonishment, the same panic.

Fama lay unconscious in a pool of blood under the bridge. The crocodile was thrashing out its death-throes in the churning water. It had all taken place in a flash; immediately afterwards, a second shot rang out. The mountains, rivers, forests and plains once more relayed the report throughout the land. The birds, animals and men reversed course; the birds soared, the men and dogs returned to the village and the beasts to the bush.

Then came a third and fourth shot, and another deafening rush of birds, animals and men.

The border guards on each side of the river were conducting a real duel. Those on the far side thought that a shot had been fired at a fugitive already on their soil. Fama was still lying under the bridge. The crocodile was flailing about in a flurry of blood and water. The shooting stopped; but the morning peace had been shattered. All Horodugu was inconsolable, because the Dumbuya dynasty was coming to an end. The dogs, the first to predict an ill-fated day, had set up a loud death-howl, without taking any notice of the stones thrown at them by the guards. The beasts of the forest roared in reply, and the crocodiles bellowed. Men prayed for the last Dumbuya, and women wept. Weaver-birds twittered in the silk-cotton and mango-trees, while vultures and hawks, high in the sky, kept watch over the uproar.

The shooting had stopped, however. The border guards of the Nikinai Republic, carrying white flags, went to fetch Fama, who lay under the part of the bridge that was within their jurisdiction. They carried him to their customs post, where their brigadier examined him; he had been mortally wounded by the crocodile.

Fama was placed in an ambulance, with the brigadier and four guards as escort. They were going to the chief town of Horodugu, beyond Togobala; so they drove off towards Togobala.

The sun was now high, very high in the sky, but Horodugu had not yet fully recovered from the shots and cries that had rent its morning. From time to time you could hear dogs howling and wild beasts roaring. But the vultures seemed once more to have settled in the trees.

The convoy started off. Two ambulance-men were sitting beside Fama. They examined him, and when they found there was no trace of a bullet-wound, they exclaimed in surprise. God is great! A sacred crocodile will attack only if it is sent by the shades to kill a transgressor of law or custom, or a great sorcerer, or a great chief. The wounded man must be someone out of the ordinary. He, Fama, was dying, amid delirious dreams. Nightmares! What nightmares!

A great heavy pain pinned down his leg.

'Quiet, keep quiet, calm down! Are you any better?' murmured the attendant on his left in a compassionate tone of voice.

Fama did not answer, his whole body had turned to stone, he felt life only in his throat that drew breath with difficulty, his nose that blew fire, his dumbfounded ears and bedazzled eyes. Outside the ambulance windows, tree-trunks, bridges, sometimes villages filed past. They were on their way. But where? Yes ... Did you not hear, Fama? You are going to Togobala, Togobala of Horodugu. Ah! here are the days you hoped for! The bastards swept away, the chiefdom restored, Horodugu is yours and your princely retinue is following you, escorting you, don't you see? Your retinue is decked in gold!

'No, not gold.'

Silver, then. Hark! what is it now? Fama, do you not see the warriors gathered round you? Fama moves forward, with the supple dignity and measured tread of a prince of Horodugu. The crowd of warriors howls, sways on the spot and stands still. Cowards! Poltroons! Children of Independence! Bastards! your mothers blossomed, but did not bear men! Fama alone will blast you with a single finger. The craven hyena herd crowds together, swarms about him; they all sing, bow down and rise like a rice-field before the wind. Fama, the One and only! The great! The strong! The virile! Sole possessor of strength and stiffness between the thighs!

He woke. Two attendants were holding him down on the stretcher. Another was shaking a hypodermic syringe. Had they given him an injection? Fama didn't know, but he could see and hear again: the motors, the lights, the jolting and dust. But did Fama, travelling towards power and glory, not dream of the moon? Is it not a fact that those whose path leads to great wealth and honour, always dream of the moon? The moon ... Fama's moon ... His moon! The moon ...

Fama on a white charger gallops, trots, leaps and prances. He is radiant and fulfilled. Praise be to the Merciful! But Fama looks back. His retinue has vanished. Where have my followers gone? he cries. He is alone, he feels loneliness closing in, it overcomes him, enters his lungs like a cloud of smoke, sears his eyes, brings on tears, empties his heart and fills his ears with nausea, until the lack, the something missing, wells up in him and bursts forth, leaving a glowing trail. Fama pursues it. Suddenly lightning flashes, shattering air, sky and earth, and the charger rears up at the edge of an abyss. Fama trembles. A prayer. Everything is all right, sweet and still and gently slipping by, the woman who comforts, and the man, there is a cool soft place under trees, fine powdery sand, and everything softens and slips away, softly and quietly, Fama is sinking, he struggles slightly one more time.

Fama had finished, was finished. They alerted the head of the convoy. They would drive on to the next village, and stop there. That village was a few miles away. Its name was Togobala. Togobala of Horodugu.

A Malinke had died. Day would follow day until the seventh day and the seventh-day funeral rites, then after a few weeks would come the fortieth day and the fortieth-day funeral rites, and ...